Georges Simenon

Maigret Loses
His Temper

Translated from the French by Robert Eglesfield

A Harvest Book • Harcourt, Inc.

A Helen and Kurt Wolff Book

Orlando   Austin   New York   San Diego   Toronto   London

www.HarcourtBooks.com

Maigret is a registered trademark of the Estate of Georges Simenon.

Library of Congress Cataloguing-in-Publication Data
Simenon, Georges, 1903–1989.
Maigret loses his temper.
(A Harvest book)
Translation of La colère de Maigret.
"A Helen and Kurt Wolff book."
I. Title.
[PZ3.S5892Mafa   1980]   [PQ2637.I53]
843'.912   80-14212
ISBN 0-15-602847-6

Printed in the United States of America
First Harvest edition 1980

A C E G I J H F D B

Maigret Loses His Temper

1

It was a quarter past twelve when Maigret passed under the perpetually cool archway and through the gate flanked by two uniformed policemen who were standing right up against the wall to obtain a little shade. He gave them a casual wave and stood for a moment motionless and undecided, glancing first toward the courtyard, then toward the Place Dauphine, then back toward the courtyard.

In the corridor upstairs, and then on the dusty staircase, he had stopped two or three times, pretending to be lighting his pipe again, in the hope that one of his colleagues or his inspectors would suddenly appear. It was unusual for the staircase to be deserted at that time, but that year, on June 2, a holiday atmosphere was already reigning at Police Headquarters.

Some people had already left at the beginning of the month to avoid the rush in July and August, and others were getting ready for the annual exodus. That particular morning, after a wet spring, the weather had suddenly turned hot, and Maigret had worked in his shirt sleeves with the windows open.

Except for his report to the Director and one or two visits to the inspectors' room, he had remained on his own. getting on with the tiresome administrative task he had begun some days before. Files piled up in front of him, and from time to time he raised his head like a schoolboy, glancing toward the motionless foliage of the trees, and listening to the hum of Paris life, which had just taken on the special quality it has on hot summer days.

For the past two weeks, he had not missed a single meal at Boulevard Richard-Lenoir and he had not been disturbed once during the evening or the night.

Normally he would have had to turn left along the Quai, in the direction of the Pont Saint-Michel, to take a bus or a taxi. The courtyard remained empty. Nobody joined him.

So, with a slight shrug of his shoulders, he turned right instead and walked into Place Dauphine, cutting across it diagonally. He had suddenly felt an urge, on leaving the office, to go to the Brasserie Dauphine and, in spite of the advice of his friend Pardon, the Rue Picpus doctor, at whose home he and Madame Maigret had dined the previous week, to treat himself to an *apéritif*.

For several weeks now he had behaved himself, making do with a glass of wine at mealtimes, and sometimes, in the evening, when he and his wife went out, a glass of beer.

Never mind! Pardon had recommended that he watch his liver, but he hadn't forbidden him to have an *apéritif*, just one, after weeks of almost total abstinence.

At the bar he found some familiar faces, at least a dozen men from Police Headquarters who had scarcely more work than he had, and who had left early. This happened at fairly long intervals: a pause lasting a few days, a dead calm, nothing but routine business, as they put it, then, all of a sudden, cases breaking at an ever-increasing rate, leaving nobody any time to draw breath.

The others nodded to him and moved up to make room for him at the bar. Pointing to the glasses filled with an opaline drink, he muttered:

"The same for me . . ."

The *patron* had already been there thirty years before,

4

when the Chief Superintendent had started at the Quai des Orfèvres, but at that time he had been the son of the owner. Now there was a son, too, wearing a chef's white hat in the kitchen, and looking like the *patron* when he had been a boy.

"How are things, Chief?"

"All right."

The smell had not changed. Every little restaurant in Paris has its particular smell, and here, for example, against a background of *apéritifs* and spirits, a connoisseur would have distinguished the rather tart scent of the plain wines of the Loire. As for the kitchen, tarragon and chives were the predominant aromas.

Maigret automatically ran his eyes over the menu on the slate: mackerel from Brittany and calf's liver *en papillottes*. At the same moment, in the dining room with its paper tablecloths, he caught sight of Lucas, who seemed to have taken refuge there, not in order to lunch, for it was not yet mealtime, but to chat in peace with somebody Maigret did not know.

Lucas now saw him, too, hesitated, got up, and came over to him.

"Have you a moment to spare, Chief? I think that this might interest you ..."

The Chief Superintendent followed him with his glass in his hand. Lucas introduced the other man:

"Antonio Farano ... Do you know him?"

The name meant nothing to the Chief Superintendent, but it seemed to him that he had already seen the handsome face of this Italian who might have been a film star. No doubt the red sports car outside the door belonged to him. It went with his appearance, with his light-colored clothes, which were rather too well cut for Maigret's taste, and with the heavy signet ring on his finger.

Lucas went on, while the three men were sitting down:

"He called at the Quai to see me just after I'd left. Lapointe told him that he might find me here . . ."

Maigret noticed that while Lucas was drinking the same *apéritif* that he was, Farano was just having fruit juice.

"He's Émile Boulay's brother-in-law. He manages one of Boulay's night clubs, the Paris-Strip, on Rue de Berri . . ."

Lucas winked discreetly at his chief.

"Repeat what you've just told me, Farano."

"Well, my brother-in-law has disappeared . . ."

He had kept his native accent.

"When?" asked Lucas.

"Last night, probably. We don't know exactly . . ."

He was overawed by Maigret, and to keep himself in countenance he took a cigarette case out of his pocket.

"Mind if I smoke?"

"Go right ahead."

Lucas explained for the Chief Superintendent's benefit:

"You know Boulay, Chief. He's that little man who arrived from Le Havre four or five years ago . . ."

"Seven years ago," corrected the Italian.

"All right, seven years ago. He bought a night club on Rue Pigalle, the Lotus, and now he owns four . . ."

Maigret wondered why Lucas wanted to involve him in this case. Since he had taken over the Crime Squad, he had rarely had anything to do with that world, which he had known very well in the old days, but now had rather lost sight of.

It was at least two years since he had last set foot in a night club. As for the criminals of Pigalle, he knew only a few of them now, mainly old hands, for that was a closed society that was constantly changing.

"I was wondering," Lucas broke in again, "whether this might have some connection with the Mazotti case . . ."

Ah! he was beginning to understand. When was it that Mazotti had been eliminated while he was coming out of a

6

bar on Rue Fontaine about three o'clock in the morning?
About a month ago. It had happened in mid-May.

Maigret remembered a report from the police in the
Ninth Arrondissement that he had passed to Lucas, saying,
"Probably a settling of old scores . . . Do what you can . . ."

Mazotti had not been an Italian, like Farano, but a Corsican who had started on the Côte d'Azur before coming up
to Paris with a little gang of his own.

"My brother-in-law didn't kill Mazotti," Farano was saying in tones of conviction. "You know very well, Monsieur
Lucas, that that isn't his line . . . Besides, you questioned
him twice in your office . . ."

"I've never accused him of killing Mazotti. I questioned
him just as I questioned everybody Mazotti had it in for
. . . That's quite a crowd . . ."

And to Maigret he added:

"As a matter of fact I sent him a summons for today at
eleven o'clock, and I was surprised not to see him . . ."

"He never sleeps out, does he?" the Chief Superintendent asked innocently.

"Never! . . . It's easy to see that you don't know him. He
isn't like that at all. He loves my sister, home life. He never
came home later than four in the morning . . ."

"And last night he didn't come home? That's it, is it?"

"That's it . . ."

"Where were you?"

"At the Paris-Strip. We didn't close till five . . . the sea-
son is in full swing for us, because Paris is already full of
tourists. Just as I was counting the takings, Marina phoned
me to ask if I'd seen Émile . . . Marina's my sister . . . I
hadn't seen my brother-in-law all night . . . He didn't often
come down to the Champs-Élysées . . ."

"Where are his other night clubs?"

"All in Montmartre, a few hundred yards from each
other. That was his idea and it paid off. With night clubs

7

more or less next door to each other, you can move your performers from one place to the next during the night and cut down on your overhead ...

"The Lotus is right at the top of Rue Pigalle, the Train Bleu practically next door, on Rue Victor-Massé, and the Saint-Trop' a little lower down, on Rue Notre-Dame-de-Lorette ...

"Émile was doubtful about opening a night club in another part of Paris, and it's the only one he didn't look after himself, you might say. He let me run it for him ..."

"So your sister phoned you shortly after five?"

"Yes. She's so used to being woken up by her husband ..."

"What did you do?"

"First of all I called the Lotus, where they told me that he had left about eleven. He also looked in at the Train Bleu, but the cashier can't say exactly when. As for the Saint-Trop', it was closed when I tried to get it on the phone."

"As far as you know, your brother-in-law didn't have an appointment last night?"

"No. As I've already said, he was a quiet man, very regular in his habits. After dinner at home ..."

"Where does he live?"

"On Rue Victor-Massé ..."

"In the same building as the Train Bleu?"

"No. Three houses farther on ... After dinner, he used to go first of all to the Lotus to supervise the preparations. That's the biggest night club and he looked after it himself ... Then he went down to the Saint-Trop', where he stayed a little while, after that to the Train Bleu, and then he started his tour all over again. He used to do it two or three times in the course of the night, because he kept an eye on everything ..."

"Was he wearing a dinner jacket?"

"No. He wore a dark suit, midnight blue, but never a dinner jacket. He didn't bother much about looking smart …"

"You talk about him in the past tense …"

"That's because something must have happened to him …"

At several tables people had begun eating, and every now and then Maigret found his gaze wandering toward the plates and the carafes of Pouilly. Although his glass was empty, he resisted the temptation to order another.

"What did you do next?"

"I went to bed, after asking my sister to ring me if there was any news."

"Did she phone you again?"

"About eight o'clock …"

"Where do you live?"

"Rue de Ponthieu."

"Are you married?"

"Yes, to an Italian girl. I spent the morning phoning the staff of the three night clubs. I was trying to find out where and when he had last been seen. It isn't as simple as you might think … for a good part of the night the clubs are packed to capacity and everybody is busy doing his job. What's more, Émile didn't stand out in a crowd … he's a skinny little man whom none of the customers ever took to be the boss, and sometimes he spent a long time outside with the doorman …"

Lucas nodded to indicate that all this was true.

"It seems that nobody saw him after half past eleven …"

"Who was the last to see him?"

"I haven't been able to question everybody … some of the waiters, barmen and musicians have no telephone. As for the girls, I don't know the addresses of most of them … I won't be able to make any serious inquiries before tonight, when everybody will be at his post. …"

"So far, the last person to have spoken to him seems to be the doorman of the Lotus, Louis Boubée, a little fellow no bigger or heavier than a jockey, and better known in Montmartre by the nickname of Mickey . . .

"Between eleven o'clock and half past eleven, Émile came out of the Lotus and stood for a while on the sidewalk near Mickey, who kept rushing forward to open the door every time a car drew up . . ."

"Did they talk to each other?"

"Émile didn't talk much. It seems that he looked at his watch several times before going off toward the bottom of the street . . . Mickey thought that he was making for the Saint-Trop' . . ."

"Has your brother-in-law got a car?"

"No. Not since the accident . . ."

"What accident?"

"It was seven years ago . . . he was still living at Le Havre, where he had a little night club, the Monaco. One day when he was driving to Rouen with his wife . . ."

"He was already married to your sister?"

"No. I'm talking about his first wife, a French girl from the country near Le Havre, Marie Pirouet. She was expecting a baby . . . in fact they were going to Rouen to consult a specialist . . . It was raining . . . The car skidded on a bend and hit a tree. Émile's wife was killed on the spot . . ."

"And what about him?"

"He got off with a gash in the cheek that left him with a scar. In Montmartre most people imagine it was done by a knife . . ."

"Did he love his wife?"

"He was crazy about her. He had known her since he was a boy . . ."

"He was born at Le Havre?"

"In a village nearby, I forget which. . . . She came from the same village. After she died, he never touched a driv-

10

ing wheel again, and as far as possible he avoided getting into a car. In Paris, for instance, he hardly ever took a taxi. He walked a lot and, when he had to, he used the Métro. Besides, he didn't like to leave the Ninth Arrondissement . . ."

"You think somebody's got rid of him?"

"All I can say is that, if nothing had happened to him, he'd have come home a long time ago . . ."

"Does he live alone with your sister?"

"No. My mother lives with them, and also my other sister, Ada, who works as his secretary . . . not to mention the two children, a boy of three, Lucien, and a little girl of ten months . . ."

"Have you any suspicions?"

Antonio shook his head.

"You think your brother-in-law's disappearance has some connection with the Mazotti case?"

"What I'm sure about is that Émile didn't kill Mazotti . . ."

Maigret turned toward Lucas, who had been in charge of the inquiry.

"What about you?"

"That's what I think too, Chief . . . I questioned him twice, and I got the impression that he was telling the truth. . . . As Antonio says, he's a puny little fellow, almost shy, not the sort you would expect to find running a set of night clubs. . . . And yet, when he had to deal with Mazotti he knew how to tackle him . . ."

"What do you mean?"

"Mazotti and his gang had organized a racket which had nothing original about it but which they'd perfected. Under the pretext of offering protection, they demanded more or less considerable sums every week from every night-club proprietor.

"Most of them, to begin with, refused to pay. Then a

well-organized little comedy was put on for their benefit. When the night club was full, Mazotti would arrive with one or two of his toughs. They would sit down at a table if there was a table free, or at the bar if there wasn't, order some champagne, and then, in the middle of a show, start a brawl. First there'd be some muttering, then voices would be raised. The barman or the headwaiter would be bawled out and called a thief....

"The whole thing would end up with glasses being broken and a more or less general free-for-all, and of course most of the customers left swearing that they'd never set foot in the place again...

"The next time Mazotti called, the owner usually decided to pay up."

"Émile didn't?"

"No. He didn't call in the local bouncers like some of his colleagues, who weren't any the better for it, because Mazotti ended up by buying them off. His idea was to send to Le Havre for a few dockers to settle Mazotti's hash."

"When was the last scrap?"

"The night Mazotti died. He'd gone to the Lotus, about one o'clock in the morning, with two of his usual pals... Émile Boulay's dockers threw them out. A few blows were exchanged..."

"Was Emile there?"

"He'd taken refuge behind the bar, because he can't bear the sight of fighting. Afterward, Mazotti went to lick his wounds in a bar on Rue Fontaine, Chez Jo, which is more or less his headquarters. There were about four or five of them drinking at the back of the bar. When they came out, at three in the morning, a car went past and Mazotti was hit by five bullets, while one of his pals got one in his shoulder. The car was never identified. Nobody talked. I questioned most of the night-club proprietors. I'm still working on the case."

"Where was Boulay when Mazotti was shot?"

"Well, Chief, as you know, it's difficult to find out anything for certain in that world. It seems that he was at the Train Bleu, but I don't put much trust in his witnesses."

"Émile didn't kill Mazotti," repeated the Italian.

"Did he carry a gun?"

"An automatic, yes . . . he had a license issued by the Police Department. That wasn't the gun that killed Mazotti."

Maigret gave a sigh and signaled to the waitress to fill up the glasses; he had been dying for another drink for quite some time.

Lucas explained:

"I wanted to put you in the picture, Chief, and I thought you'd be interested to hear what Antonio had to say . . ."

"I've told you nothing but the truth . . ."

Lucas went on:

"I summoned Émile to the Quai for this morning. I must admit it worries me that he disappeared last night of all nights . . ."

"What did you want to ask him?"

"It was just routine. I was going to ask him the same questions as last time, to check with his first answers and with the other affidavits . . ."

"The two occasions you had him in your office did he seem frightened?"

"No. Irritated, rather. Above all else he wanted to keep his name out of the papers. He kept saying that it would do tremendous harm to his business, that his night clubs were well run, that nothing unlawful ever happened in them, and that if his name was mentioned in connection with a settling of scores, he would never get over it . . ."

"That's right," said Antonio approvingly, making as if to get up.

He added:

"You don't need me any more, do you? I've got to join my sisters and my mother, who are in a terrible state . . ."

A few moments later, they heard the roar of the red car shooting off toward the Pont-Neuf. Maigret took a slow sip of his *apéritif*, darted a sidelong glance at Lucas, and sighed:

"Are you expected anywhere?"

"No. I was thinking of . . ."

"Eating here?"

And, as he nodded, Maigret decided:

"In that case, we'll have a meal together. I'll call my wife . . . You go ahead and order."

"Would you like some mackerel?"

"Yes, and some calf's liver *en papillottes* . . ."

It was the calf's liver which tempted him most of all, together with the atmosphere of the brasserie where he hadn't set foot in weeks.

The case was not terribly important, and so far Lucas had looked after it by himself. Nobody, outside of the underworld, was concerned about Mazotti's death. Everybody knew that that sort of settling of scores was always cleared up in the end, even if by another killing.

The best about those cases was that the Public Prosecutor's Department and the examining magistrates were not constantly spurring the police on to find the culprit. As one magistrate put it:

"It means one less to be given board and lodging for years in prison. . . ."

The two men chatted together as they ate. Maigret learned a little more about Émile Boulay and ended up by getting interested in that curious little man.

The son of a Norman fisherman, Émile, at the age of sixteen, had signed on as a steward with the Compagnie Transatlantique. That had been before the war. He was in

New York as a member of the crew of the *Normandie* when hostilities broke out in France.

How had such a puny man come to be accepted by the American Marines? He had spent the war with them before going back into service, this time as a deputy chief steward, on the *Ile-de-France*.

"You know, Chief, that nearly all of them dream of setting up on their own, and after two years of marriage Boulay bought a bar in Le Havre, which he turned into a dance hall before long. Striptease was just beginning at the time, and it seems that he had soon made quite a pile. . . .

"When the accident happened, and his wife was killed, he was already planning to extend his activities to Paris . . ."

"Did he keep the night club in Le Havre?"

"He put a manager in. One of his old pals on the *Ile-de-France* runs it for him. . . .

"In Paris he bought the Lotus, which wasn't doing as well as it is now. It was a second-rate joint, a tourist trap like dozens of others round the Place Pigalle."

"Where did he meet Antonio's sister?"

"At the Lotus. She was working in the cloakroom. She was only eighteen."

"What was Antonio doing at that time?"

"He was a worker at Renault, in the body assembly shop. He had been the first to arrive in France. Then he had sent for his mother and his two sisters. They lived in the Javel district."

"In fact, Émile seems to have more or less married the whole family. . . . Did you go and see him at home?"

"No. I had a look at the Lotus and his other night clubs, but I didn't think it necessary to go to his apartment."

"You're sure he didn't kill Mazotti?"

"Why should he have killed Mazotti? He was winning the game . . ."

"He might have been frightened . . ."

"Nobody in Montmartre thinks he did it . . ."

They drank their coffee in silence and Maigret refused the Calvados which the *patron* came to offer him as usual. He had drunk two *apéritifs,* and after that only a single glass of Pouilly, so that, walking back to Police Headquarters with Lucas, he felt reasonably pleased with himself.

In his office he took off his jacket, loosened his tie, and set to work on the administrative files. It was a question of nothing less than a complete reorganization of all the police services, on which he'd been asked to prepare a report, and he was applying himself to the task like a conscientious student.

In the course of the afternoon his thoughts occasionally went to Émile Boulay, to the little Montmartre empire which the former steward with the Compagnie Transatlantique had built up, to the young Italian with the red car, and to the apartment on Rue Victor-Massé where the three women lived with the children.

During this time Lucas was phoning the hospitals and the various police stations. He had also issued a description of Boulay, but by half past six these inquiries had not produced any results.

The evening was almost as hot as the day had been, and Maigret went for a walk with his wife, spending nearly an hour over a single glass of beer at the table outside a café on Place de la République.

They talked mainly about the holidays. A good many of the passers-by were carrying their jackets over one arm, and most of the women were wearing printed cotton dresses.

The next day was a Thursday. Another glorious day. The night reports did not mention Émile Boulay, and Lucas had no news.

There was a violent but short-lived storm about eleven o'clock, after which steam seemed to be rising from the roadway. He went home for lunch, and then came back to his office and the pile of files.

When he left the Quai des Orfèvres, there was still no news of the little man from Le Havre, and Lucas had spent a fruitless afternoon in Montmartre.

"It does seem, Chief, that it's Boubée, the man they call Mickey and who's been the doorman at the Lotus for years, who was the last to see him. He thinks he remembers seeing Émile turn the corner of Rue Pigalle and Rue Notre-Dame-de-Lorette as if he was making for the Saint-Trop', but he didn't attach any importance to it. . . . I'll go back to Montmartre tonight, when everybody'll be at his post."

Lucas was to discover nothing more. At nine o'clock on Friday morning Maigret had just finished looking through the daily reports when he called Lucas into his office.

"They've found him," he announced, lighting his pipe.

"Alive?"

"Dead."

"In Montmartre? In the Seine?"

Maigret held out a report from the Twentieth Arrondissement. It stated that a corpse had been found at daybreak on Rue des Rondeaux, just outside the Père Lachaise cemetery. The body was lying across the sidewalk, not far from the railway embankment. It was dressed in a dark blue suit, and in the wallet, which contained a fair amount of money, there was an identity card in the name of Émile Boulay.

Lucas looked up, frowning.

"I wonder . . ." he began.

"Go on reading."

The rest was in fact calculated to astonish the inspector even more. The report went on to state that the corpse, which had been taken to the Forensic Laboratory, was in a state of advanced decomposition.

Admittedly, not many people went along that part of Rue des Rondeaux, which was a dead end. All the same, a corpse could not have remained on the sidewalk there for two days, or even a few hours, without being detected.

"What do you think about it?"

"It's very odd . . ."

"Have you read it all?"

"Not the last few lines . . ."

Émile Boulay had disappeared sometime between Tuesday night and the early hours of Wednesday morning. Given the state of the body, it was probable that he had been killed in that period.

Two whole days had gone by, two days of considerable heat.

It was hard to understand what reason the murderer or murderers could have had for keeping the body all that time.

"Now that's even stranger!" exclaimed Lucas, putting the report on the desk.

The strangest thing in fact was that, according to the first examination, the crime had not been committed with a firearm, or with a knife either.

As far as could be ascertained, pending the post-mortem, Émile Boulay had been strangled.

Now neither Maigret nor Lucas, despite their long years of service in the police, could remember a single crime in the underworld committed by strangulation.

Every district in Paris, every social class, has, so to speak, its own way of killing, just as it has its own method of committing suicide. There are streets where you throw yourself out of the window, others where you turn on the gas, and still others where you take an overdose of barbiturates.

The police know the knifing districts, those where bludgeons are used and those, like Montmartre, where firearms are preferred.

Not only had the little night-club owner been strangled, but, for two days and three nights, the murderer had kept the body.

Maigret was already opening the cupboard to get his jacket and his hat.

"Let's go!" he growled.

At last he had an excuse to leave his administrative assignment.

In fine June weather, cooled by a light breeze, the two men made for the Forensic Laboratory.

2

The pink buildings of the Forensic Laboratory, on the Quai de la Rapée, look more like a laboratory for pharmaceutical products than the old mortuary under the big clock of the Palais de Justice.

Behind a desk in a well-lighted office, Maigret and Lucas found an employee who recognized them straightaway and said with a polite smile:

"I suppose it's about the fellow from Rue des Rondeaux?"

The electric clock above his head gave the time as five past ten, and through the window they could see the barges on the other side of the Seine moored in front of the warehouse docks.

"There's somebody waiting there already," continued the official, who appeared to want to make conversation. "It seems he's a relative . . ."

"Did he give his name?"

"I'll ask him for it when he's identified the body and comes here to sign his declaration."

The man's concern with the corpse was purely theoretical, in the form of cards in a card index.

"Where is he?"

"In the waiting room . . . I'm afraid you'll have to wait, too, Monsieur Maigret . . . Dr. Morel is in the middle of his work. . . ."

The corridor was white, with a light-colored floor, and the waiting room was bright, too, with its two benches and its chairs in polished wood, and its big table, which only lacked a few magazines to make you think you were at the dentist's. The walls, coated with oil paint, were bare; Maigret had often wondered what sort of pictures or engravings they could have hung on them.

Antonio was sitting on one of the chairs, his chin in his hands, and although he still looked handsome, his face was a little puffy, like that of a man who has not had enough sleep; his cheeks were unshaven.

He stood up as the police officers came in.

"Have you seen him?" he asked.

"Not yet."

"I haven't either. I've been waiting over a half an hour. It's Émile's identity card all right that they showed me . . ."

"Who?"

"An inspector with a queer name . . . wait a minute . . . Mornique? . . . Bornique?"

"Yes, Bornique . . ."

Maigret and Lucas exchanged glances. This was bound to happen with Bornique of the Twentieth Arrondissement. There were a few like him in the district police stations—not only inspectors but Chief Superintendents, too—who insisted on competing with Police Headquarters and who made it their business to arrive before the men from the Quai des Orfèvres.

Maigret had only learned about the finding of the body from the daily reports, and since the discovery the men of the Twentieth Arrondissement had not been idle. It was precisely to avoid this sort of excessive zeal that Maigret had been working for several weeks on a reorganization of the police force.

"Do you think the doc's going to be much longer? The women are nearly crazy . . ."

"Was it Bornique who went and told them?"

"It was before eight o'clock this morning. They'd just got up and were seeing to the kids.

" 'Which of you is called Marina Boulay?' " he asked.

"Then he held out an identity card to my sister.

" 'That's your husband's card, isn't it? Do you recognize his photograph? When did you last see him?'

"You can imagine the scene. Ada phoned me straight-away. I was asleep. I didn't stop to have breakfast or even make myself a cup of coffee. A few minutes later, I was in Rue Victor-Massé and the inspector all but treated me as a suspect.

" 'Who are you?'

" 'The brother-in-law . . .'

" 'This lady's?'

" 'No. Her husband's . . .' "

Antonio's nerves were still on edge.

"I had to argue for a long time before he agreed to let me come and identify the body instead of my sister. She insisted on coming with me. As I guessed it wouldn't be very pretty, I made her stay at home . . ."

He nervously lighted a cigarette.

"The inspector didn't come with you?"

"No. It seems he's got other things to do. He told me that the clerk here would give me a form to fill out and sign . . ."

After a pause he added:

"You see that I was right to feel worried. The day before yesterday you looked as if you didn't believe me. Where is it, Rue des Rondeaux?"

"It runs alongside the Père Lachaise cemetery."

"I don't know that part of Paris. What sort of district is it?"

A door opened. Dr. Morel, in a white smock, his cap on his head and a gauze mask hanging under his chin, looked around for the Chief Superintendent.

"I've just been told you were waiting to see me, Maigret.
. . . Would you like to come along?"

He led them into a room where the only light came in
through frosted-glass panes and where the walls were
lined with metal cabinets, as in an office, with the difference that the cabinets were of an unusual size. A body,
covered with a cloth, was stretched out on a cart.

"His brother-in-law had better identify him first," said
the Chief Superintendent.

With the traditional gesture, the sheet was drawn away
from the face. The dead man's features had been invaded
by a beard a quarter of an inch long, and reddish in color,
like his hair. The skin had a blue tint here and there, and
on the left cheek the scar which Antonio had mentioned
at the Brasserie Dauphine stood out clearly.

As for the body, it looked slight and thin under the sheet.

"It's him all right?"

"Yes, of course it's him . . ."

Sensing that the Italian was feeling sick, Maigret sent
him to the office with Lucas to attend to the formalities.

"Can we put him away?" asked the doctor, motioning to
a man in a gray smock who had already opened one of the
drawers. "Will you come with me, Maigret?"

He took him into an office equipped with a washbasin
and, while he was speaking, disinfected his hands and face,
took off his white smock, and reassumed the appearance
of an ordinary man.

"I suppose you'd like a few details to be getting on with
until I send in my report? As usual, we'll have to make
some analyses that will take several days. What I can tell
you right now is that the body shows no signs of any
wounds. The man was strangled or, to be more precise . . ."
Morel was searching for words, as if he wasn't too sure of
himself.

"This isn't official, you understand . . . I won't be so dogmatic in my report. . . . If I had to reconstruct the murder in the light of the post-mortem, I would say that the victim was attacked from behind, that the murderer put an arm around his neck and pulled so sharply that a cervical vertebra was broken . . ."

"So he was standing up?"

"Standing up, or just possibly seated . . . I personally think that he was standing and that he wasn't expecting this attack . . . there was no real struggle . . . he didn't put up a fight. I examined his fingernails carefully, and I didn't find any shreds of wool in them, as there would have been if he had clawed at his attacker's clothes. Nor did I find any blood or hairs, and there weren't any scratches on his hands either. Who is he?"

"A night-club owner. Have you any idea when he was killed?"

"Two full days at least, three at the most, have elapsed since the man died, and I might add one detail, still off the record: in my opinion the body wasn't exposed to the open air during that period. You'll be getting a preliminary report this evening . . ."

Lucas reappeared.

"He's signed the papers. . . . What shall I do with him? Shall I let him go back to Rue Victor-Massé?"

Maigret nodded, because he still had to examine Émile's clothes and the contents of his pockets. Later in the day this task would be done again, more scientifically, in the laboratory.

The things were in another room, piled up on a table. The dark-blue suit was not torn anywhere and there was only a little dust on it. There was no blood. It was scarcely rumpled. As for the black shoes, they were as clean as those of a man who has just left home, with just a couple of recent scratches on the leather.

Maigret would have been willing to bet that the crime

had not been committed in the street but in a house, and the murderer had got rid of the body by leaving it on the sidewalk of Rue des Rondeaux, only toward the end of the previous night.

Where had it been brought from? The murderer had almost certainly used a car. The corpse had not been dragged along the sidewalk.

As for the contents of the pockets, they were rather disappointing. Had Émile Boulay been a smoker? It seemed not. There was no pipe, no cigarettes, no lighter or matches. Nor any of those shreds of tobacco you always find in the bottom of a smoker's pockets.

A gold watch. In the wallet, five hundred-franc notes and three fifties. The ten-franc notes were loose in one of the pockets, and in the other there was some small change.

A bunch of keys, a penknife, a crumpled handkerchief, and, in the breast pocket, another handkerchief, neatly folded. A small bottle of aspirin tablets and some peppermints.

Lucas, who was emptying the wallet, exclaimed:

"Look! My summons . . ."

A summons that Émile Boulay would have found it difficult to comply with . . .

"I thought he was in the habit of carrying an automatic," growled Maigret.

The firearm was not among the objects spread out on the table, but there was a checkbook, which the Chief Superintendent looked through. It was practically new. Only three checks had been drawn. The only large one was for five thousand francs and made out to "self."

The stub was dated May 22 and Lucas observed right away:

"That's funny! That's the day I summoned him for the second time to the Quai des Orfèvres. I'd seen him there the first time on the eighteenth, the day after Mazotti's death..."

"Will you phone the lab to come and get these things and examine them?"

A few minutes later the two men got back into the car, which Lucas drove with prudent slowness.

"Where are we going, Chief?"

"First of all to Rue des Rondeaux . . . I want to see the place where he was found. . . ."

In the sunshine, in spite of the cemetery and the railway, the place did not look sinister. From some way off they could see a few sight-seers being kept at bay by a couple of policemen, some housewives at their windows, and some children playing. When the car stopped, Maigret was greeted by Inspector Bornique, who said with an air of false modesty:

"I was expecting you, Chief Superintendent. I thought you'd be coming and I was careful to . . ."

The policemen stood to one side, revealing the silhouette of a body drawn in chalk on the grayish sidewalk.

"Who found him?"

"An employee of the gas company who goes on duty at five o'clock in the morning and who lives in that house over there . . . that's his wife you can see at the third-floor window. I've got his statement of course. It so happened that I was on night duty . . ."

It was not the moment, with the sight-seers there, to rebuke him.

"Tell me, Bornique, did you get the impression that the body had been thrown out of a car or that it had been put on the sidewalk?"

"That it had been put on the sidewalk . . ."

"On its back?"

"No, face down . . . at first sight, you'd have taken it for a drunk who was sleeping it off . . . except for the smell.

". . . Because I must say, the smell . . ."

"I suppose you've questioned the neighbors?"

"All those that are at home . . . mainly women and old men, because the younger men have gone off to work . . ."

"Nobody saw anything or heard anything?"

"Only an old woman, up there on the fifth floor, who suffers from insomnia, so it seems. It's true that her concierge says that she doesn't know what she's talking about any more. . . . She says that about half past three this morning she heard the brakes of a car . . . they don't get many in this part of the street, which doesn't lead anywhere . . ."

"She didn't hear any voices?"

"No. Just a car door opening, then some footsteps, then the door shutting again."

"She didn't look out the window?"

"She's practically bedridden. Her first idea was that there was somebody ill in the house and they'd sent for an ambulance. She waited to hear the door open and shut, but the car went off almost immediately, after making a turn in the street . . ."

Inspector Bornique added, as a man who knows his job:

"I'll be coming back at noon and this evening, when the men are home from work."

"Has the Public Prosecutor been here?"

"Very early. He didn't stay long. It was just a formality . . ."

Watched by the sight-seers, Maigret and Lucas got back into the car.

"Rue Victor-Massé . . ."

Piles of cherries and some early peaches could be seen on the peddlers' pushcarts with housewives circling around them. Paris was very gay that morning, with more passersby on the shady sidewalks than on those exposed to the sun.

In Rue Notre-Dame-de-Lorette they caught sight of the yellow front of the Saint-Trop', whose entrance was closed by an iron grille; on the left of the door was a frame containing photographs of nudes.

On Rue Victor-Massé an almost identical frame showed on the longer façade of the Train Bleu, and Lucas drew up a little farther on, outside a middle-class house. It was a grayish building, fairly prosperous-looking, and a couple of brass plates announced the names, one of a doctor, the other of a building society.

"What is it?" asked a rather disagreeable concierge, opening her glass door.

"Madame Boulay . . ."

"Third floor on the left, but . . ."

After looking at the two men, she changed her tone.

"You're from the police, aren't you? . . . In that case you can go up. . . . Those poor women must be in an awful state . . ."

There was an almost silent elevator and a red carpet on the staircase, which was better lighted than in most of the old apartment houses in Paris. On the third floor they could hear voices behind a door. Maigret rang the bell and the voices stopped, footsteps drew near, and Antonio appeared in the doorway. He had taken off his jacket and was holding a sandwich.

"Come in . . . don't take any notice of the mess . . ."

A baby was crying in a bedroom. A little boy was clinging to the dress of a young woman who was already fairly plump. She had not had time to do her hair, which hung down her back.

"My sister Marina . . ."

She was red-eyed, as was only to be expected, and looked somewhat distraught.

"Come this way . . ."

She took them into an untidy living room. There was

a rocking horse overturned on the carpet and some dirty cups and glasses on the table.

An old, much fatter woman in a baby-blue dressing gown appeared at another door and looked suspiciously at the newcomers.

"My mother," said Antonio, introducing her. "She speaks hardly any French . . . she'll never get used to it . . ."

The apartment was huge and comfortable, equipped with the rustic furniture that you find in the big stores.

"Where's your other sister?" asked Maigret, looking around him.

"With the baby . . . she'll be coming soon . . ."

"How do you explain all this, Chief Superintendent?" asked Marina, who had less of an accent than her brother.

She had been eighteen or nineteen when Boulay had met her. That meant she was twenty-five or twenty-six now, and she was still very beautiful, with a mat complexion and dark eyes. Had she kept her pride in her appearance? It was not easy to judge in the circumstances, but the Chief Superintendent would have been willing to bet that she had stopped bothering about her figure or her clothes, that she'd been living happily with her mother, her sister, her children, and her husband, without bothering about the rest of the world.

As soon as he had come in, Maigret had sniffed the air, recognizing the smell of the place; it reminded him of Italian restaurants.

Antonio had obviously become the head of the family. Hadn't he rather occupied that position in the time of Émile Boulay? Hadn't it been he whom the former steward had had to ask for Marina's hand?

Still holding his sandwich, he asked:

"Have you discovered anything?"

"I'd like to know if he had his automatic in his pocket when he went out on Tuesday night."

Antonio glanced at his sister, who hesitated for a moment and then rushed into another room. She left the door open, revealing the dining room, which she crossed before going into a bedroom. She opened a drawer and came back with a dark object in her hand.

It was the automatic, which she handled gingerly, like someone who is frightened of firearms.

"It was in its usual place," she said.

"He didn't always carry it on him?"

"Not always, no . . . not recently . . ."

Antonio broke in.

"After Mazotti was killed and his gang went back to the South, Émile didn't feel the need to be armed any more . . ."

That was a significant point. It meant that when he had left home on Tuesday evening, Émile Boulay hadn't been expecting a dangerous or delicate encounter.

"At what time did he leave you, madame?"

"A few minutes before nine, as usual. We had dinner at eight. Then he went to kiss the children good night in their beds, as he always did before going out . . ."

"He didn't strike you as being worried?"

She made an effort to remember. She had very beautiful eyes, which, under normal circumstances, must have been gay and caressing.

"No . . . I don't think so. You know, Émile wasn't at all demonstrative, and people who didn't know him must have imagined that he was very reserved . . ."

Tears came to her eyes.

"In reality he was very kind, very attentive. . . ."

She turned toward her mother, who was listening, her hands folded over her stomach, and said a few words to her in Italian. Her mother nodded in confirmation.

"I know what they think about people who run night clubs. They think they're some kind of gangsters and it's true there are a few like that . . ."

She wiped her eyes, and looked at her brother as if to ask his permission to go on.

"But he was timid if anything . . . perhaps not in business matters . . . He lived in the midst of dozens of women he could have done what he liked with, but instead of treating them as most of his colleagues do, he regarded them as employees, and if he was strict with them, he was also respectful. I know that because I worked for him before becoming his wife . . .

"You can believe me or not, as you like, but he spent weeks circling around me like a young man would have done. When he spoke to me during the show, it was to ask me questions: where I was born, where my family lived, whether my mother was in Paris, whether I had any brothers and sisters . . .

"Not once, during all that time, did he touch me. Nor did he ever offer to take me home."

Antonio nodded, with a look that implied he wouldn't have allowed anything else to happen.

"Of course," she went on, "he knew what Italian girls were like, because there are always two or three at the Lotus. One evening, he asked me if he could meet my brother . . ."

"He did the right thing," conceded Antonio.

The mother must have understood a little French, and now and then she opened her mouth as if she were going to break in. But, failing to find the words she wanted, she ended up by keeping quiet.

A girl came in, dressed in black, with her hair already done and her face freshly made up. This was Ada, who was barely twenty-two and obviously looked just as her sister had at that age. She glanced inquisitively at the visitors and told Marina:

"She's finally gone off to sleep."

Then she said to Maigret and Lucas:

"Won't you sit down?"

"I understand, mademoiselle, that you were your brother-in-law's secretary?"

She, too, had the merest hint of an accent—just enough to give her an added charm.

"That's saying a lot. Émile looked after all his business himself. And it's the sort of business that doesn't require a lot of paper work."

"Did he have an office?"

"We call it the office anyway . . . two little rooms on the mezzanine, over the Lotus . . ."

"When did he go there?"

"He usually slept till noon and had lunch with us. About three o'clock the two of us went over to the Place Pigalle. . . ."

Maigret observed the two sisters one after the other, wondering whether, for instance, Marina might not feel a certain jealousy of her younger sister. He found no trace of any such feeling in her eyes.

Marina, as far as he could judge, had, only three days before, been a woman content with her lot, happy leading a fairly lazy life with her mother and her children in the Rue Victor-Massé apartment, and probably, if her husband had not been killed, she would have had a large family.

Very different, with a more energetic, clear-cut personality, Ada went on:

"There were always some people waiting—show girls, musicians, the headwaiter or the barman of one night club or another, not to mention the travelers in wines and champagne . . ."

"What did Émile Boulay attend to on the day he disappeared?"

"Wait a minute . . . it was Tuesday, wasn't it? . . . We went down to the club to audition a Spanish dancer,

32

whom he took on. . . . Then he saw the representative of an air-conditioning firm. He was planning to install air-conditioning in his four night clubs. At the Lotus in particular they kept having trouble with the ventilation . . ."

Maigret remembered a catalogue he had noticed among the dead man's effects.

"Who looks after his financial affairs?"

"What do you mean?"

"Who paid the bills, the staff?"

"The accountant, of course . . ."

"Did he have an office over the Lotus, too?"

"Yes, a little room overlooking the yard. He's an old man who's always grumbling, and whenever there's any money to be spent, it hurts him as if it were his own. He's called Raison . . . Monsieur Raison, as everybody says, because if they didn't call him monsieur . . ."

"Is he at the Place Pigalle now?"

"Yes. He's the only one who works in the morning, because he's free in the evening and all night."

"I suppose that each night club has its own manager?"

Ada shook her head.

"No. It doesn't work like that. Antonio runs the Paris-Strip because it's in another part of Paris with a different clientele and a different style. You understand what I mean? Besides, Antonio is one of the family . . .

"The other three night clubs are practically next door to one another. In the course of the night some of the performers go from one to another. Émile, too, circulated between them and kept an eye on everything. About three o'clock in the morning we'd sometimes send some crates of champagne from the Lotus to the Train Bleu, or some bottles of whisky. If one of the clubs was crowded and short of staff, we'd send reinforcements from another club where there were fewer people . . ."

"In other words, Émile Boulay ran the three Mont-martre night clubs in person."

"More or less . . . although in each club there was a headwaiter who was in charge."

"And Monsieur Raison looked after the accounts and the paperwork . . ."

"That's about it."

"And you?"

"I followed my brother-in-law around and took notes—a reminder to order this or that, to make an appointment with such and such a tradesman or such and such a contractor, to ring up a girl who was working somewhere else to try and book her . . ."

"Did you follow him around in the evening, too?"

"Only part of the evening."

"Till what time, usually?"

"Ten or eleven. The longest job was getting everything ready about nine o'clock. There's always somebody missing, a waiter, a musician, or a dancer. Or else there's a delivery of champagne or party favors that is late . . ."

Maigret said thoughtfully:

"I'm beginning to get the hang of it. . . . Were you with him on Tuesday evening?"

"Yes, like every evening . . ."

He glanced again at Marina and found no trace of jealousy in her face.

"At what time did you leave your brother-in-law?"

"At half past ten."

"Where were you at the time?"

"At the Lotus. It was a sort of headquarters . . . we'd already dropped into the Train Bleu and the Saint-Trop'."

"You didn't notice anything special?"

"No, nothing . . . except that I thought it was going to rain."

"Did it rain?"

"A few drops, just as I was leaving the Lotus. Mickey offered to lend me an umbrella, but I hung around and five minutes later the rain stopped."

"Did you make a note of Boulay's appointments?"

"I reminded him about them if necessary. It wasn't often necessary, because he thought of everything. . . . He was a calm, thoughtful man, who ran his business seriously."

"He didn't have an appointment that particular evening?"

"Not as far as I know . . ."

"Would you have known?"

"I suppose so . . . I don't want to make myself out to have been more important than I was. For instance, he never discussed his business or his plans with me, but he talked about them in front of me. When he saw people I was nearly always there. I don't remember him asking me to leave the room once. He'd say things to me like:

" 'We'll have to change the curtains in the Train Bleu.'

"I'd make a note of it and remind him about it the following afternoon."

"What was his reaction when he heard that Mazotti had been killed?"

"I wasn't there at the time. He must have heard about it during the night, like the whole of Montmartre, because that sort of news travels fast."

"And the next day, when he got up?"

"He asked me for the papers right away . . . I went to buy them for him at the corner."

"You mean he wasn't in the habit of reading the papers?"

"He'd just glance at one morning paper and the evening one."

"Did he play the horses?"

"Never . . . neither horses, nor cards, nor any sort of game."

"Did he talk to you about Mazotti's death?"

"He told me that he expected to be summoned by the police and got me to phone the headwaiter at the Lotus to find out if the police had already called there."

Maigret turned toward Lucas, who understood his silent query.

"Two inspectors from the Ninth Arrondissement went there," he said.

"Did Boulay seem worried?"

"He was afraid of getting some unfavorable publicity . . ."

It was Antonio's turn to enter the conversation.

"That was always his big worry. He often told me to see that my place was decently run.

" 'Just because we earn our living showing naked women,' he used to say, 'that doesn't mean we're gangsters . . . I'm a respectable businessman and I want people to know it. . . .' "

"That's right . . . I've heard him say the same thing. But you're not drinking, Chief Superintendent."

Although he had no desire for Chianti at half past eleven in the morning, he moistened his lips all the same.

"Had he any friends?"

Ada looked around, as if that in itself were an answer.

"He hadn't any need of friends. His life was here."

"Did he speak Italian?"

"Italian, English, and a little Spanish . . . he learned them on the transatlantic liners, and then in the United States."

"Did he ever talk about his first wife?"

Marina showed no embarrassment while her sister replied:

"He visited her grave every year and her picture is still on the bedroom wall."

"One more question, Mademoiselle Ada. When he died,

Boulay had a checkbook in his pocket. Did you know about that?"

"Yes. He always had it on him, but he didn't use it much. The big payments were made by Monsieur Raison. Émile always had a wad of bank notes in his pocket, too. That's necessary in the business."

"Your brother-in-law was summoned to Police Headquarters on May 18 . . ."

"I remember . . ."

"Did you go with him to the Quai des Orfèvres?"

"As far as the door . . . I waited for him on the sidewalk . . ."

"Did you take a taxi?"

"He didn't like taxis or cars in general. We went by Métro."

"Later he received a summons for May 23 . . ."

"I know. . . . It annoyed him."

"Still because of the publicity?"

"Yes."

"Now, on May 22 he drew quite a large sum—five thousand francs—out of the bank. Did you know that?"

"No."

"You didn't look after his checkbook?"

She shook her head.

"Did he prevent you from seeing it?"

"No. It was his personal checkbook and it never occurred to me to open it. He didn't lock it up, and left it lying about on the bureau in his bedroom . . ."

"Did he ever draw large sums out of the bank?"

"I doubt it. It wasn't necessary. When he needed some money, he took it out of the till at the Lotus or one of the other night clubs and left a note in its place."

"You've no idea why he should have drawn all that money?"

"None at all."

"You've no means of finding out?"

"I can try . . . I can ask Monsieur Raison. I can look through his correspondence . . ."

"Will you be good enough to do that today and call me if you discover anything?"

On the landing, Antonio, looking rather embarrassed, asked a question.

"What do we do about the night clubs?"

And as Maigret looked at him uncomprehendingly, he made his meaning clearer:

"Do we open them in spite of everything?"

"Personally, I can see no reason for . . . But I imagine that's a matter for your sister to decide, isn't it?"

"If we close them, people are going to wonder . . ."

Maigret and Lucas got into the elevator, which had just stopped at that floor, leaving the Italian perplexed.

3

On the sidewalk, Maigret lighted his pipe, blinking his eyes
in the sunshine, and was just going to speak to Lucas when
a little scene that was typical of Montmartre life unfolded
before them. The Train Bleu was not far away, its neon
sign extinguished and its shutters closed. Right opposite
the Boulays' house, a young woman rushed out of a little
hotel, wearing a black evening dress, with a tulle scarf
around her bare shoulders. In the daylight her hair was of
two different colors and she had not bothered to renew
her make-up.

She was tall and slim, with the build of a music-hall
dancer. Running across the street on extremely high heels,
she went into a little bar, where she was probably going to
have a cup of coffee and some croissants.

Another person came out of the hotel practically at her
heels, a man between forty-five and fifty, the northern
businessman type, who, after glancing right and left, made
for the corner and hailed a taxi.

Maigret automatically looked up at the windows of the
third floor of the house he had just left, and the apartment where three women, together with two children,
had constructed a little Italy of their own.

"It's a quarter past eleven. I've got a good mind to go
and see Monsieur Raison in his office. While I'm doing that
you might ask a few questions in the district, especially

in the shops, at the butcher's, the dairy shop, and so on."

"Where shall I meet you again, Chief?"

"Why not Chez Jo?"

The bar where Mazotti had been shot. Maigret wasn't following any definite plan. He had no ideas. He was rather like a retriever running around sniffing all over the place. And to tell the truth, he was not averse to savoring once more that Montmartre air, which he had not breathed for years.

He turned the corner of Rue Pigalle and stopped outside the grille across the Lotus doorway, looking for a bell button that wasn't there. The door behind the grille was shut. Next to it there was another night club, smaller and rather shabby in appearance, with its façade painted an aggressive mauve, then the narrow window of a lingerie shop in which some extraordinary panties and brassières were displayed.

On the off-chance he went into the hallway of an apartment house and found a shrewish concierge in her lodge.

"The Lotus?" he asked.

"Can't you see that it's closed?"

She looked at him suspiciously, possibly scenting the policeman in him.

"It's the accountant I want to see—Monsieur Raison . . ."

"The staircase on the left in the yard . . ."

A dark, narrow yard, cluttered with garbage pails overlooked by windows that, for the most part, had no curtains. A brown door stood half open, leading to an even darker old staircase, whose steps creaked under Maigret's weight. On one of the doors on the mezzanine there was a zinc plate with some words crudely stamped on it: "The Full Moon." This was the name of the club next door to Émile's.

Opposite there was a cardboard notice: "The Lotus." Maigret had the disillusioning impression of going into a theater by the stage door. The dull, dusty, almost shabby surroundings evoked no idea of evening dresses, or of naked bodies, or of champagne and music.

He knocked, heard nothing, knocked again, and finally decided to turn the enamel handle. He found himself in a narrow corridor where the paint was flaking off the walls, with a door in front of him and another on his right. It was on this latter door that he knocked again, and at the same time he heard a scuffling sound. He was kept waiting for quite a while before a voice said:

"Come in . . ."

He found a little sunlight filtering through dirty windowpanes, and a fat man of indeterminate age, but fairly old, with a few gray hairs brushed back over his bald head, who was straightening his tie while a young woman in a print dress stood by trying to look unconcerned.

"Monsieur Raison?"

"That's me," replied the man, avoiding his eyes.

The Chief Superintendent had obviously disturbed them.

"Chief Superintendent Maigret."

The atmosphere in the room was stifling, and there was a scent of heady perfume.

"I'm off, Monsieur Jules. Don't forget what I asked you for . . ."

Looking embarrassed, he opened a drawer and, from a worn, stuffed wallet he took two or three bank notes, which he held out to her.

They disappeared in a flash into the girl's handbag, and she went off on her stiletto heels.

"They're all the same," sighed Monsieur Raison, wiping his face with his handkerchief, possibly for fear that some traces of lipstick were visible.

"They're paid on Saturday and as early as Wednesday they come and ask you for an advance. . ."

An odd sort of office and an odd sort of man! You wouldn't have thought you were behind the scenes in a night club, but rather in a more or less shabby den. There were no photographs of girls on the walls, as you might have expected, but a calendar, some metal filing cabinets, and some shelves loaded with files. The furniture could have been bought in a junk shop, and the chair Monsieur Raison offered the Chief Superintendent had one leg mended with a piece of string.

"Have you found him?"

The accountant had not quite yet recovered his composure. His hairy hand trembled slightly while he was lighting a cigarette, and Maigret noticed that his fingers were stained with nicotine.

In this office, which overlooked the yard, you could hear hardly anything of the noise of the street, except perhaps a vague hum. You were in another world. Monsieur Raison was in shirt sleeves, with large patches of sweat under his arms, and his stubbly face was covered with sweat, too.

Maigret would have been willing to bet that he was not married, that he had no relatives, and that he lived on his own in some gloomy room in the district, cooking his meals on a hot plate.

"Have you found him?" he repeated. "Is he alive?"

"Dead . . ."

Monsieur Raison sighed and piously lowered his eyelids.

"I guessed as much. What happened to him?"

"Strangled . . ."

He raised his head abruptly, as surprised as the Chief Superintendent had been at the Quai de la Rapée.

"Does his wife know? . . . And Antonio?"

"I've just come from Rue Victor-Massé . . . Antonio has identified the body. . . . I should like you to answer one or two questions."

"I'll answer them as best I can."

"Do you know if Émile Boulay had any enemies?"

The teeth were yellow; Monsieur Raison must have bad breath.

"That depends on what you mean by enemies. Business rivals, yes . . . he was doing too well for some people's liking. . . . It's a difficult business, where the going is tough."

"How do you account for the fact that within a few years Boulay was able to buy four night clubs?"

The accountant was beginning to feel better, and now he was on familiar ground.

"If you want my opinion, it's because Monsieur Émile looked after them like he'd have looked after, say, a chain of grocery stores. He was a serious-minded man."

"You mean that he didn't consume his own wares?" said the Chief Superintendent, unable to resist the temptation to be sarcastic.

The other man registered the hit.

"If you're thinking of Léa, you're wrong. She treats me like her father. They nearly all come here to tell me their secrets and their little troubles . . ."

"And ask you for an advance. If I've understood it correctly, Boulay's only relations with them were those of an employer with his employees?"

"That's right. He loved his wife and family. He didn't put on a tough act, and he didn't have a car, or a house in the country or by the sea. He didn't throw his money around or try to impress anybody. That's pretty rare in this racket. He'd have been a success in any line of business. . . ."

"So his rivals were jealous of him?"

"Not to the extent of killing him. . . . As for the underworld, Monsieur Émile had succeeded in winning their respect."

"Thanks to his dockers."

"You mean the Mazotti business? I can assure you that he had nothing to do with the murder. He simply refused to pay, and to settle those gentlemen's hash he sent for a few toughs from Le Havre. That was enough . . ."

"Where are they now?"

"They went back home a fortnight ago. The inspector in charge of the case gave them permission to leave Paris . . ."

He was talking about Lucas.

"Boulay was anxious to keep on the right side of the law . . . you can ask your colleague in the Vice Squad, who's in Montmartre nearly every night and knows what's what . . ."

An idea occurred to Maigret.

"Would you mind if I use the phone?"

He dialed the home number of Dr. Morel, whom he had forgotten to ask one question that morning.

"Tell me, Doctor, is it possible, before the results of the analyses come through, for you to tell me roughly how long after dinner Boulay was killed? . . . What? . . . No, I'm not asking for a precise answer . . . To the nearest hour, yes. . . . I know that, judging by the contents of the stomach, he had had dinner at eight in the evening . . . What's that you say? . . . Between midnight and one o'clock in the morning? Thank you."

That was one small point that had been settled.

"I suppose, Monsieur Raison, that you don't work in the evening?"

The accountant shook his head, almost indignantly.

"I never set foot in a night club. That isn't my job . . ."

"I imagine your boss kept you informed about his business affairs?"

"Theoretically, yes."

"Why theoretically?"

"Because, for instance, he didn't talk to me about his plans. When he bought Paris-Strip, to put his brother-in-

44

law in there, I knew about it only the day before the papers were signed. He wasn't a talkative man."

"He didn't say anthing to you about any appointment on Tuesday evening?"

"Not a thing . . . I'd better try to explain to you how the place works. I'm here in the morning and afternoon. In the morning, I'm nearly always on my own. In the afternoon the boss used to come along with Ada, who acted as his secretary . . ."

"Where's his office?"

"I'll show you . . ."

It was at the end of the corridor, and it was hardly any bigger or more luxurious than the office the two men had just left. In one corner there was a desk with a typewriter on it. A few filing cabinets. On the walls, photographs of Marina and the two children. Another photograph of a woman, a blonde with sad eyes, whom Maigret assumed to be Boulay's first wife.

"He called me only when he needed me. I did nothing but place orders and settle bills."

"So it was you who saw to all the payments. Including the direct payments, I suppose?"

"What do you mean?"

Although Maigret had never belonged to the Vice Squad, he was familiar with night life in Paris all the same.

"I imagine that certain payments were made in cash, without any receipt, if only to dodge the Internal Revenue . . ."

"You're wrong about that, Monsieur Maigret, if you'll allow me to contradict you. . . . I know that's the idea everybody has about the business, and it sounds easy . . . but where Monsieur Boulay was different from all the rest was that he insisted, as I've already said, on keeping on the right side of the law."

"Did you do his income tax returns?"

"Yes and no. I kept his accounts up to date and I handed them over, when the time came, to his lawyer . . ."

"Let's suppose that at a given moment Boulay needed a fairly large sum, five thousand francs . . ."

"That's easy. He'd have taken them out of the till in one of the night clubs and left a note in their place . . ."

"Did that ever happen to him?"

"Not for any sum as large as that . . . A thousand, perhaps . . . two thousand . . ."

"So he had no need to go and draw money out of the bank?"

This time Monsieur Raison hesitated before answering, intrigued by the question.

"Wait a minute. . . . In the morning I'm here, and there's always a tidy sum in the safe. It's only about noon that I go to the bank to pay in the previous night's receipts. . . . Besides, I've practically never seen him in the office in the morning, because he was usually still asleep. In the evening, as I've already said, he only had to dip into the till of the Lotus, the Train Bleu or the Saint-Trop'. The afternoon was a different matter. If he had needed five thousand in the middle of the afternoon, he would probably have dropped into the bank . . ."

"That's what he did on May 22. Does that date mean anything to you?"

"Not a thing . . ."

"You've no trace of a payment made that day or the following day?"

They had returned to Monsieur Raison's office, and the accountant was consulting a register bound in black cloth.

"Nothing," he said.

"You're sure your boss didn't have a girl friend?"

"In my opinion that's quite out of the question . . ."

"Nobody was blackmailing him? Can you check from

46

his bank statements whether Boulay drew any other checks in the same way?"

The accountant went to take a file out of one of the cabinets. He ran his pencil down the columns.

"Nothing in April . . . or in March . . . or in February. Nothing in January either . . ."

"That will do. . . ."

So on one occasion only in the course of the past few months, Émile Boulay had drawn some money in person out of the bank. That check continued to bother the Chief Superintendent. He sensed that something was escaping him, something that was probably important, and his thoughts went round and round.

He came back to a question he had already asked.

"You're sure your boss didn't make any direct payments?"

"I can't see what he'd have paid for that way . . . I know it's hard to believe, but you can ask Maître Gaillard. . . . On that point Monsieur Émile was almost a maniac. He maintained that it's precisely when you're in a rather dubious business that you've got to be most straightforward . . .

"Don't forget that everybody's suspicious of us, that we've got the police on our tracks all the time, not just the Vice Squad, but the Fraud Squad, too. . . .

"Talking about the Fraud Squad, I remember a story. Two years ago, at the Saint-Trop', an inspector found some rather strange whisky in brand-name bottles. . . .

"I don't need to tell you that that sort of thing goes on in a good many places. . . . Naturally the excise people started proceedings. Monsieur Émile swore he didn't know anything about it. . . . His lawyer looked into it. They were able to prove that it was the barman who was working the switch for his own profit.

"The boss fixed things up all the same, but I don't need to tell you that the barman was sacked.

47

"Another time I saw him in an even greater fury. He'd noticed some suspicious characters among the customers of the Train Bleu. . . . When you're used to the clients, you can spot right away the people who aren't there for the same reasons as the others, you understand?

"On that occasion the police didn't have to intervene . . . Monsieur Émile found out before they did that a musician he'd recently taken on was trafficking in drugs, on a small scale, incidentally . . ."

"And he fired him?"

"That very night."

"How long ago was that?"

"It was before the case of the barman, about three years ago . . ."

"What became of the musician?"

"He left France a few weeks later and he's working in Italy."

Nothing in all this explained the five thousand francs, still less the death of Boulay, whom somebody had kept for two days and three nights, heaven knows where, before leaving him on an empty street alongside the wall of Père Lachaise.

"Are these offices connected in any way with the night club?"

"This way . . ."

He opened a door that Maigret had taken for that of a cupboard. He had to switch on a light, for it was almost completely dark, and Maigret saw a steep spiral staircase in front of him.

"Do you want to go downstairs?"

"Why not?"

He followed Monsieur Raison down the staircase, which ended in a room where women's clothes, some of them covered with sequins or imitation pearls, were hung along the walls. There was a dressing table painted gray and littered with jars of cream, paints, and pencils. A sweetish, slightly sickening smell hung in the air.

It was here that the dancers changed out of their everyday clothes into their professional trappings before displaying themselves under the glare of the spotlights, where men bought champagne at five or six times its price for the privilege of admiring them.

But first they had to cross, as Monsieur Raison and Maigret did now, a sort of kitchen separating the dressing room from the club.

Two or three thin rays of light were filtering through the shutters. The walls were mauve, the floor covered with paper streamers and multicolored cotton balls. The smell of champagne and tobacco remained, and there was still a broken glass in one corner, near the orchestra's instruments, which were wrapped in their covers.

"The cleaners don't come until the afternoon. They are the same women who do the cleaning at the Train Bleu. At five o'clock they go to the Rue Notre-Dame-de-Lorette, so that by nine o'clock everything's ready to welcome the customers...."

It was as depressing as, say, a seaside resort in winter, with its villas and its casino closed. Maigret looked around him, as if the setting were going to give him an idea, a starting point.

"Can I get straight out from here?"

"The key of the grille is upstairs, but if you insist . . ."

"No, don't bother."

He climbed the staircase again, only to go down the one into the yard a little later, after shaking Monsieur Raison by his moist hand.

It was a pleasure, after that, to be bumped into by a boy running along the sidewalk, and to breathe in the good, healthy smell of a vegetable stall.

He was familiar with the bar run by Jo, whom everybody called Jo the Wrestler. He had known it for at least twenty years, if not longer, and the bar had had a great many owners. Perhaps this was because of its strategic position—a stone's throw from Place Pigalle, Place Blanche, and the sidewalks, which a crowd of women paced tirelessly up and down all night.

Closed down a score of times by the police, the bar had nonetheless always become a meeting place for the local criminals again. And, even before Mazotti, some of them had been killed there.

Yet the place looked peaceful enough, at this time of day at least. It presented the traditional appearance of all Paris bistros, with its bar, its mirrors on the wall, its benches, and, in one corner, four cardplayers; two plasterers in smocks, their faces smudged with white, were drinking wine at the counter.

Lucas was already there, and the *patron*, a colossus with his shirt sleeves rolled up, told him as he saw the Chief Superintendent come in:

"Here's your boss! . . . What can I serve you, Monsieur Maigret?"

He kept his sarcastic expression throughout the most ticklish interrogations, and he had undergone a fair number in his career, which incidentally included no convictions.

"A glass of white wine."

Lucas's face told him that the inspector had discovered nothing important. Maigret was not disappointed. He was still in the period when, as he used to say, he was putting himself in the picture.

The four cardplayers shot a glance at him now and then, in which there was more irony than fear. There was also a certain irony in Jo's voice when he asked:

"So you've found him?"

"Who?"

"Come, come, Chief Superintendent . . . you're forgetting you're in Montmartre, where news travels fast. If Émile disappeared three days ago and we see you prowling around the district . . ."

"What do you know about Émile?"

"Me?"

Jo the Wrestler liked playing the fool.

"What could I know? Is a gentleman like him, a virtuous businessman, likely to set foot in my establishment?"

This produced smiles in the cardplayers' corner, but the Chief Superintendent drew on his pipe and drank his wine without getting annoyed. Then he announced in a serious voice:

"He's been found . . ."

"In the Seine?"

"No, as it happens, not in the Seine . . . I could almost say he was found in the cemetery . . ."

"He wanted to save himself the cost of a funeral. That wouldn't surprise me with him. . . . But joking apart, Émile's dead?"

"Yes. Dead three days."

This time, Jo frowned just as Maigret had done that morning.

"You mean to say he died three days ago and he wasn't found until this morning?"

"Stretched out on the sidewalk on Rue des Rondeaux . . ."

"Where's that?"

"I've already told you . . . a dead end, running alongside Père Lachaise."

The cardplayers pricked up their ears, and he could tell that they were as surprised as the boss.

"But he can't have been there three days?"

"He was put there last night . . ."

"Then if you want my opinion, I'd say there's something fishy about that. It's fairly hot just now, isn't it? And there's no joy in keeping a stiff around the place in this sort of weather. . . . Not to mention the fact that that's a queer district to leave that sort of parcel. Unless it's a nut who's done the job . . ."

"Tell me, Jo, can you talk seriously for a moment?"

"Dead serious, Monsieur Maigret."

"Mazotti was killed coming out of your bar . . ."

"Just my luck! I'm beginning to wonder whether he didn't do it on purpose to get my license taken away . . ."

"You'll have noticed that we haven't bothered you."

"Except that I've spent three mornings with your inspector," retorted Jo, jerking his head toward Lucas.

"I'm not going to ask you if you know who did it . . ."

"I didn't see a thing . . . I'd gone down to the cellar to get some bottles."

"I don't care whether that's true or not. In your opinion, could Émile Boulay have done the killing?"

Jo had turned serious, and, to give himself time to think, he poured himself a glass of wine, taking the opportunity to fill those of Maigret and Lucas. He also darted a glance toward the cardplayers' table, as if he wanted to ask their advice or to get them to understand his position.

"Why ask *me* that question?"

"Because you are one of the men who knows most about what goes on in Montmartre . . ."

"That's just what people say. . . ."

He was flattered all the same.

"Émile wasn't a real professional," he murmered in the end, almost regretfully.

"You didn't like him?"

"That's another matter. Personally, I had nothing against him."

"And the others?"

"What others?"

"His rivals. I've heard that he was planning to buy some more night clubs . . ."

"And why not?"

Maigret returned to his starting point.

"Would Boulay have been capable of killing Mazotti?"

"I've told you he wasn't a professional. The Mazotti business was a professional job. You know that as well as I do. His dockers wouldn't have tackled it that way either . . ."

"Second question . . ."

"How many are there?"

"This may be the last."

The plasterers were listening, exchanging winks.

"Shoot! I'll see if I can answer."

"You've just admitted that Émile's success didn't please everybody . . ."

"A fellow's success never pleases other people . . ."

"Only this is a world where they play a cautious game and where the seats are dear . . ."

"Granted. What next?"

"Do you think Émile was killed by a colleague?"

"I've already answered that one, too."

"When?"

"Didn't I say that there was no joy in having a corpse on your hands for two or three days, especially in this sort of weather? Let's suppose the people you're talking about are sensitive. Or else that they're so closely watched that they daren't take any risks. How was he killed?"

In any case the story would be in the afternoon papers.

"Strangled."

"Then the answer is even more definite, and you know why. Mazotti's killing was a clean job. If the people around here had wanted to get rid of Émile, they'd have done it in the same way. Have you found the people who killed Mazotti? No! And in spite of all your informers, you won't get them. Whereas this story of yours about a man who's strangled, who's kept indoors for three days, and who's dumped by a cemetery wall—well, it smells, that's all I can say. So much for your second question . . ."

"Thank you."

"You're welcome. Have another?"

He held the bottle inquiringly over the glass.

"Not this morning . . ."

"Don't tell me you're thinking of coming back. I've got nothing against you personally, but in this business we prefer not to see too much of you."

"How much is it?"

"The second round is on me. The day he spent three hours questioning me, your inspector treated me to a glass of beer and a sandwich. . . ."

Outside, Maigret and Lucas said nothing for a long time. At one moment Maigret raised his arm to stop a taxi and the inspector had to remind him that they'd come in a car from Police Headquarters. They found it again and got in.

"Home," growled Maigret.

He had no serious reason for lunching out. To tell the truth, he had no idea yet how to tackle the case. Jo the Wrestler had only confirmed what he'd been thinking ever since that morning, and he knew that Jo had been sincere.

It was true that Émile Boulay was a nonprofessional who had paradoxically dug himself in right in the middle of Montmartre.

And, oddly enough, it seemed that he had been killed by another nonprofessional.

"What about you?" he asked Lucas.

The inspector understood what he meant.

"The three women are well known to all the local shop-keepers. They call them the Italian women. They make fun a bit of the old woman and her broken French. They don't know Ada so well, because she doesn't often go shopping, but they used to see her passing with her brother-in-law.

"The people I've been questioning don't know the news

54

yet. The family seems to like eating well. . . . According to the butcher, it's amazing what they can put away, and they always insist on the best cuts of meat. Every afternoon, Marina goes for a walk around the Square d'Anvers, pushing the baby carriage with one hand and holding the little boy with the other . . ."

"They haven't got a maid?"

"Just a cleaning woman three times a week."

"Have you got her name and address?"

Lucas blushed.

"I can get them this afternoon."

"What else do they say?"

"The fishmonger's wife said to me:

" ' He's as smart as they come . . .'

"She was talking about Émile, of course.

" 'He married the eldest when she was nineteen. When he saw that she was beginning to spread, he sent for her young sister . . . I bet he'll find another sister or a cousin in Italy when Ada gets fat in her turn. . . .' "

That had occurred to Maigret, too. It wasn't the first time he had seen a husband in love with his sister-in-law.

"Try to find out some more about Ada . . . what I'd particularly like to know is whether she has a boy friend or a lover . . ."

"Is that what you think, Chief?"

"No. But we mustn't neglect anything. I'd like to know some more about Antonio, too. It might be a good idea if you went around to Rue Ponthieu this afternoon."

"All right."

Lucas stopped the car in front of the apartment house where Maigret lived, and, looking up, the Chief Superintendent saw his wife leaning on the balcony rail. She gave him a little wave. He waved back and went into the building.

4

When the telephone rang, Maigret, who had his mouth full, motioned to his wife to answer it.

"Hello . . . Who's that speaking? . . . Yes, he's having lunch . . . I'll call him. . . ."

He looked at her, frowning and bad-tempered.

"It's Lecoin . . ."

He got up, still chewing, taking his napkin with him to wipe his mouth. For the last five minutes, as it happened, he had been thinking about his colleague Lecoin, the chief of the Vice Squad, whom he had decided to call on during the afternoon. Maigret's contacts with the underworld of Montmartre, and of Pigalle in particular, went rather a long way back, whereas Lecoin was up to date.

"Hello . . . Yes, I'm listening . . . No, of course not . . . That doesn't matter . . . I was thinking of coming to see you this afternoon . . ."

The chief of the Vice Squad, who was about ten years younger than Maigret, lived quite close to Boulevard Richard-Lenoir, on Boulevard Voltaire, in an apartment that was always noisy, for he had six or seven children.

"I've got somebody here whom you are sure to know," he explained. "He's been one of my informers for a long time now. He prefers not to show his face at the Quai, and when he has something to tell me, he comes to see me at home. . . . Now it happens that today his tip concerns you

56

rather than me. Of course, I don't know what it's worth. . . .
As for the fellow himself, apart from the frills he likes to
add because he's an artist in his way, you can trust him."

"Who is it?"

"Louis Boubée, alias Mickey, the doorman at a night
club in Montmartre."

"Send him over right away."

"You're sure you don't mind him coming over to your
place?"

Maigret finished his lunch quickly; when the doorbell
rang, his wife had just poured his coffee, which he took
with him into the living room.

He had not seen the man nicknamed Mickey for several
years, but he recognized him at once. He could scarcely
have failed to do so, for Boubée was a rather extraordinary
creature. How old would he be now? The Chief Superintendent tried to work it out. He had still been a fairly
young inspector when his visitor was already working as a
doorman in Montmartre.

Boubée had not grown any taller. He was still the size
of a child of twelve or thirteen, and the most extraordinary
thing about him was that he still looked like a child, too.
A skinny little boy, with big projecting ears, a long pointed
nose, and a grinning mouth that you might have thought
was made of India rubber.

You had to look closer to see that his face was covered
with tiny wrinkles.

"Quite a time since we last met, isn't it?" he said, looking
around him, with his cap in his hand. "You remember the
Tripoli and La Tétoune?"

The two men must have been the same age, to within
two or three years.

"Those were the good old days, weren't they!"

He was referring to a now defunct brasserie on Rue
Duperré, a stone's throw from the Lotus, and which,

before the war, just like its proprietress, had had its hour of fame.

La Tétoune was a portly Marseillaise reputed to do the best southern cooking in Paris and who was in the habit of greeting her customers with smacking kisses and speaking to them familiarly.

It was a tradition when you arrived to go and see her in her kitchen, and you met an unusual set of customers in her restaurant.

"You remember Fat Louis, who owned the three brothels on Rue de Provence? And One-eyed Eugène? And Handsome Fernand, who ended up in the movies?"

Maigret knew that it was useless asking Mickey to come to the point. It was a matter of honor with him; he was quite prepared to give information to the police, but in his own way, without appearing to do so.

The men he was talking about were the big bosses of the underworld of their day, the owners of brothels that still existed, and they used to meet at La Tétoune's. They rubbed shoulders there with their lawyers, for the most part leading attorneys; as the place became fashionable, you also met actresses there and even members of the Cabinet.

"In those days, I used to take bets on boxing matches. ..."

Another peculiar thing about Mickey was the absence of eyelashes and eyebrows, which made him look decidedly odd.

"Since you've become the big chief of the Crime Squad, we scarcely ever see you in Montmartre. . . . Monsieur Lecoin, of course, comes there now and then. Sometimes I can do him a good turn, as I used to with you in the old days. You hear so many things, you know...."

What he did not add was that it was essential for him that the police should shut their eyes to certain activities of his. The clients of the Lotus who gave him a tip as they came out of the club never suspected that Mickey was also in business on his own.

He sometimes whispered in the ear of one of them:

"Animated pictures, monsieur?"

He could say that in a dozen languages, with a meaning wink. After which he would slip into the client's hand a card bearing the address of a nearby apartment.

It was not really very wicked. What you saw there in great secrecy was roughly the same spectacle, though in dustier, more sordid surroundings, as was offered by any Pigalle night club. With the difference that the women were no longer twenty, but often at least twice as old.

"Your inspector, the little fat one . . ."

"Lucas . . ."

"Yes . . . he called me in about three weeks ago, after Mazotti was killed, but I didn't know very much . . ."

He was gradually coming to the point, in his own way.

"I told him it definitely wasn't my boss who'd done the job, and I wasn't wrong. Now I've got a tip. You've always been pretty understanding with me, so I'll give it to you, for what it's worth, of course . . . I'm not talking to the police, get that straight . . . I'm talking to a man I've known a long time. We're just having a little chat. By accident we just happen to start talking about Mazotti, who, between ourselves, wasn't up to much. . . .

"Then I just repeat what somebody told me . . . it's no use looking in Pigalle for the guy who did the job. At Easter . . . when was Easter this year?"

"At the end of March . . ."

"Good. Well then, at Easter, Mazotti, who was nothing at all, but who wanted people to think he was a big shot, a real man, went down to Toulon. There he met Yolande . . . you know her? . . . She's Mattei's woman. Mattei is the boss of the False Noses of Marseilles, who pulled off about twenty holdups before they got copped. You're with me so far?

"Mattei was in jail, and Mazotti, who thought he could do what he liked, came back to Paris with Yolande . . . I don't need to say any more, do I? . . . There are still a few of Mattei's men in Marseilles, and two or three of them came up to Paris to settle things . . ."

It was plausible. A professional job, with no hitches.

"I thought that would interest you, and not knowing your address, I went to see your pals . . ."

Mickey showed no signs of taking his leave, which meant that he had not said all that he wanted to say or that he was expecting to be asked some questions. Sure enough, Maigret asked him with an innocent air:

"Have you heard the news?"

"What news?" Mickey asked with a similar air of innocence.

And immediately he gave a mischievous smile.

"You mean about Monsieur Émile? I heard he'd been found . . ."

"Have you just been around to Jo's place?"

"We're not great friends, Jo and me, but the news has got around."

"What has happened to Émile Boulay interests me more than the Mazotti business. . . ."

"Well, in that case, Chief Superintendent, I've got to admit that I don't know a thing . . . and that's the truth I'm telling you."

"What did you think of him?"

"What I said to Monsieur Lucas . . .what everybody thinks . . ."

"And that is?"

"He ran his business his own way, but he kept on the right side of the law."

"Do you remember Tuesday evening?"

"I've a pretty good memory . . ."

He kept smiling all the time, as if each of his words deserved to be emphasized, and he had a mania for winking.

"Nothing special happened?"

"That depends on what you regard as special. . . . Monsieur Émile came along about nine o'clock with Mademoiselle Ada to see if everything was ready, like he did every night . . . you know how it is. . . . Then he dropped into the Train Bleu and he went around to Rue Notre-Dame-de-Lorette, too . . ."

"What time did you see him again?"

"Wait a minute. The orchestra had started playing . . . that means it must have been after ten. . . . The club was practically empty. You can make as much noise as you like to attract clients but they don't start coming in until after the movies and theaters are closed . . ."

"Did his secretary stay with him?"

"No. She went off home."

"Did you see her going into the apartment house?"

"I think I followed her with my eyes, because she's a pretty kid and I always give her a bit of the soft talk, but I couldn't swear to it . . ."

"And what about Boulay?"

"He went into the Lotus to make a phone call."

"How do you know he made a phone call?"

"Germaine, the cloakroom girl, told me so . . . the phone is near the cloakroom. The box has a glass door. He dialed a number and got no answer, and when he came out he looked annoyed."

"Why did that strike the cloakroom girl?"

"Because usually, when he made a phone call in the evening, it was to one of his night clubs, or to his brother-in-law, and he always got an answer. Besides, a quarter of an hour later, he tried again."

"Still without success?"

"Yes . . . so he was calling somebody who wasn't at home, and that seemed to irritate him. Between the calls, he went and prowled around the club. He had a word with a dancer whose dress was dirty and he chewed out the barman.

"After a third or fourth try, he came out on the sidewalk for a breath of fresh air . . ."

"Did he speak to you?"

"He wasn't a talkative man, you know. . . . He just planted himself like that in front of the door. He looked at the sky and the traffic and he might say whether we'd have a full house or not . . ."

"Did he finally get an answer?"

"Yes, about eleven o'clock."

"And he went off?"

"Not right away. He came back out to the sidewalk . . . that was one of his habits. . . . Two or three times, I saw him take his watch out of his pocket. Finally, after twenty minutes or so, he started walking down Rue Pigalle . . ."

"In other words, he had an appointment . . ."

"I see we've got the same idea . . ."

"It seems he scarcely ever took a taxi . . ."

"That's right. After his accident, he didn't like cars. He preferred the Métro."

"You're sure he went down Rue Pigalle? Not up?"

"Certain!"

"If he'd been going to take the Métro, he would have gone up the street . . ."

"That's what he did when he went to have a look at Rue de Berri . . ."

"So that in all probability his appointment was in the neighborhood . . ."

"First of all I thought he was going to the Saint-Trop', on Rue Notre-Dame-de-Lorette, but nobody saw him there."

"Do you think he had a mistress?"

"I'm sure he didn't."

And, with another wink, the wizened little boy added:

"After all, I know something about it . . . I'm in the business, in a manner of speaking, aren't I?"

"Where does Monsieur Raison live?"

The question surprised Mickey.

"The accountant? He has lived for at least thirty years in the same apartment house, on Boulevard Rochechouart."

"Alone?"

"Of course! . . . He hasn't a mistress either, believe me. . . . It isn't that he doesn't like women, but his income doesn't match his tastes, and he just messes about with the girls who come to his office to ask for an advance . . ."

"You know what he does in the evening?"

"He plays billiards, always in the same café, on the corner of the Square d'Anvers. There aren't many billiard tables left in the neighborhood. He's practically a champion."

Another line of inquiry which seemed to have come to a dead end. Maigret went on asking questions all the same, not wanting to leave anything to chance.

"Where does this Monsieur Raison come from?"

"From a bank. He was a cashier, for I don't know how many years, at the branch where the boss had his account, on Rue Blanche. I suppose he gave him a few tips. Monsieur Émile needed somebody reliable to do the bookkeeping, because in that business there's plenty of waste. I don't know how much he pays him, but it must be quite a lot, seeing that Monsieur Raison left the bank . . ."

Maigret kept coming back to the Tuesday evening. It was becoming an obsession. By now he could see before him little Monsieur Émile standing under the neon sign of the Lotus, looking at his watch now and then and finally setting off in a determined way down Rue Pigalle.

He was not going far, otherwise he would have taken the Métro, which was only a hundred yards away. If he had needed a taxi, in spite of his dislike for cars, there were always plenty driving past his night club.

A sort of map began to take shape in Maigret's mind, the map of a small part of Paris to which everything kept bringing him back. The former steward's three night clubs were close to one another, and only the Paris-Strip, which was run by Antonio, was an exception.

Boulay and his three Italian women lived on Rue Victor-Massé. Jo the Wrestler's bar, outside which Mazotti had been shot, could almost be seen from the entrance of the Lotus.

The bank where Émile had his account was barely farther away, and finally the accountant, too, lived in the neighborhood.

It was rather like a village, which Émile Boulay left only rarely, and regretfully.

"You've no idea who the person might be he had an appointment with?"

"No, honest I haven't . . ."

After a pause Mickey admitted:

"I've thought about it, too, just out of curiosity . . . I'd like to understand. In my business, it's essential to understand, isn't it?"

Maigret got up with a sigh. He could think of no other questions he ought to ask. The doorman had told him a certain number of details of which he had been ignorant, and of which he might have remained ignorant for a long time, but these details still did not explain Boulay's death, and even less the almost incredible fact that somebody had kept his body for three nights and two whole days before leaving it next to Père Lachaise.

"Thank you, Boubée . . ."

Just as he was going out, the little man said:

"You're not still interested in boxing, are you?"

"Why?"

"Because I've got a tip about a fight tomorrow, if you like to . . ."

"No, thanks . . ."

He did not give him any money. It was not for money that Mickey sold his services, but in exchange for a certain indulgence.

"If I hear anything, I'll give you a ring. . . ."

Three quarters of an hour later, in his office at Police Headquarters, Maigret scribbled on a sheet of paper, rang the bell in the inspector's room, and sent for Lapointe.

Lapointe did not need to look twice at the Chief to know how far he'd got. Nowhere! He had the dazed, obstinate look he always had at the worst period of an investigation, when he did not know how to tackle it and struck out, without much confidence, in all directions.

"Go to Boulevard Rochechouart and check up on a certain Monsieur Raison . . . he's the accountant at the Lotus and the other night clubs belonging to Émile Boulay. . . . It seems that he plays billiards every evening in a café on the Square d'Anvers. I don't know which, but you'll find it. Try to find out as much as you can about him and his habits. . . . Above all, I'd like to know whether he was at the café on Tuesday evening, what time he left, and what time he reached home . . ."

"I'm on my way, Chief . . ."

Lucas, in the meantime, was checking up on Ada and also Antonio. Maigret, to calm his impatience, plunged into his administrative files. About half past four, he had had enough of them and, putting on his jacket, he went out to have a beer by himself at the Brasserie Dauphine. He nearly ordered a second, not because he was thirsty, but to defy his friend Pardon, who had advised abstinence.

He hated not understanding. It was becoming a personal

matter for him. He kept coming back to the same pictures: Émile Boulay, in a blue suit, standing outside the Lotus, going back into the night club, telephoning, getting no reply, walking around and around, and telephoning again and yet again under the impassive gaze of the cloakroom girl.

Ada had gone home. Antonio was attending to the first customers on Rue de Berri. In the four night clubs, the barmen were arranging their glasses and bottles, the musicians were tuning their instruments, and the girls were getting ready in sordid dressing rooms before taking their places in front of the little tables.

Finally Boulay obtained his number, but he did not leave right away. So the appointment was not immediate. He'd been given a particular time.

He stood waiting outside the club again, took his watch out of his pocket several times, and then, all of a sudden, walked down Rue Pigalle . . .

He had had dinner at eight o'clock. According to the police doctor, he had been killed four or five hours later, in other words between midnight and one o'clock in the morning.

When he had left the Lotus, it had been half past eleven.

He had had between half an hour and an hour and a half to live.

It was known that he had had nothing to do with Mazotti's death. The remaining members of the Corsican's gang were well aware of this and had no reason to kill him.

Finally, nobody in the underworld would have done the job as Émile's murderer had, strangling him, keeping his body for two days, and then running the risk of taking it to Rue des Rondeaux . . .

Ada was not aware of any appointment of her employer's. Nor was Monsieur Raison. Antonio maintained that he knew nothing either. Even Mickey, who had good reasons for finding out about everything that was going on, was in the dark on this point.

Maigret was pacing up and down his office in a state of irritation, the stem of his pipe clenched between his teeth, when Lucas knocked on the door. The inspector was not exhibiting the triumphant expression of somebody who had just made a discovery.

Maigret just looked at him and said nothing.

"I don't know much more than I did this morning, Chief . . . except that Antonio didn't leave his night club on Tuesday evening, or at any time during the night . . ."

Of course not! That would have been too easy.

"I've seen his wife, an Italian woman who's expecting a baby. . . . They live in a smart apartment on Rue de Ponthieu . . ."

The Chief Superintendent's vacant gaze made Lucas feel uneasy.

"It isn't my fault . . . Everybody likes them . . . I spoke to the concierge, the tradesmen, and the night club's neighbors. . . . Then I went back to Rue Victor-Massé. I found the accountant in his office and asked him for the addresses of the performers who work at the Lotus and do their turns in the other clubs. . . . Two of them were still asleep in the same hotel . . ."

He felt as if he were talking to a wall, and now and then Maigret turned his back on him to watch the Seine flowing by.

"Another girl, who lives on Rue Lepic, has a baby and . . ."

The Chief Superintendent looked so irritable that Lucas got flustered.

"I can only tell you what I know. They are all more or less jealous of Ada, of course. . . . They've got the impression that sooner or later she'd have become the boss's mistress, but that it hadn't happened yet . . . Not to mention the fact that Antonio, so it seems, would have raised objections . . ."

"Is that all?"

Lucas spread his hands in a gesture of discouragement.

"What shall I do now?"

"Whatever you like."

Maigret went home early, after studying that tedious business of the reorganization of the police services a little longer; he felt sure it would not be carried out along the lines he was suggesting.

Reports, always reports! They asked his advice. They begged him to draw up a detailed plan. Then it all came to a halt somewhere in the administrative hierarchy and nothing more was heard about it. Unless, of course, they made arrangements contrary to those he had proposed.

"I'm going out tonight," he told his wife in a grumpy voice.

She knew that it was better not to ask him any questions. He sat down for supper and watched television, growling from time to time:

"It's too damn stupid!"

Then he went into the bedroom to change his shirt and tie.

"I don't know when I'll be back . . . I'm going to Montmartre to visit a few night clubs . . ."

You would have thought that he was trying to make her jealous, and that he was annoyed to see her smile.

"You ought to take your umbrella . . . the radio says there are going to be some thunderstorms."

To tell the truth, if he was in a bad temper, it was because he had the impression that it was his fault that he was in the dark. He was sure that at a certain moment during the day—he could not have said precisely when—he had been on the point of getting on the right track.

Somebody had said something significant to him. But who? He had seen so many people!

It was nine o'clock when he took a taxi, and twenty past nine when he arrived outside the Lotus, where Mickey greeted him with a conspiratorial wink and opened the red velvet door for him.

The musicians in their white dinner jackets were not yet in their places, and were chatting in a corner. The barman was wiping glasses on his shelf. A lovely redhead with a very low-cut dress was filing her nails at one end of the room.

Nobody asked him what he had come for, as if they all knew all about it. They just kept darting inquisitive glances at him.

The waiters were putting ice buckets on the tables. Ada, in a dark suit, came out of the back room with pencil and notebook, caught sight of Maigret, and, after hesitating for a moment, came toward him.

"My brother advised me to open the clubs," she explained with a certain embarrassment. "The fact is, none of us knows what we ought to do. . . . It seems that it isn't usual to close when there is a death in the family . . ."

Glancing at the notebook and pencil, he asked her:

"What were you doing?"

"What my brother-in-law used to do every evening at this time . . . checking the stocks of champagne and whisky with the barmen and headwaiters . . . Then organizing the moves of the performers from one night club to another . . . they're never all there. . . . Every day you have to make some last-minute changes. I've been around to the Train Bleu . . ."

"How is your sister?"

"She's very dejected. Luckily, Antonio spent the afternoon with us. The undertaker's men came by . . . they're due to bring the body back home tomorrow morning. . . .

The telephone never stopped ringing. And then we had to see about the invitations to the funeral . . ."

She remained very calm, and, while talking to Maigret, she kept an eye on the preparations, just as Boulay would have done. She even broke off to say to a young waiter:

"No, Germain . . . no ice in the buckets yet . . ."

A new man, probably . . .

Maigret asked at random:

"Did he leave a will?"

"We don't know, and that complicates matters because we don't know what arrangements to make."

"Did he have a legal adviser?"

"Only his lawyer, Maître Jean-Charles Gaillard, but he isn't at home. He left early this morning for Poitiers, where he has a case, and he won't be back until late tonight."

Who was it who had already mentioned a lawyer? Maigret searched his memory, and found the rather unappetizing picture of Monsieur Raison in his little mezzanine office. What had they been talking about at that moment? Maigret had asked if certain payments were not made direct in order to avoid taxation.

He remembered now the trend of the conversation. The accountant had maintained that Monsieur Émile had not been a man to cheat the Internal Revenue and risk trouble, that he had insisted on everything being aboveboard and that his income tax returns had been prepared by his lawyer . . .

"You think it's to him that your brother-in-law would have gone about his will?"

"He asked his advice about everything . . . Don't forget that, when he started, he knew nothing about business. When he opened the Train Bleu, some neighbors sued him, I can't remember why . . . probably because the music prevented them from sleeping."

"Where does he live?"

"Maître Gaillard? On Rue La Bruyère, in a small private house about halfway up the street . . ."

Rue La Bruyère! Barely five hundred yards from the Lotus. To get there you simply had to go down the Rue Pigalle, cross Rue Notre-Dame de Lorette, and, a little farther down, turn to the left.

"Did your brother-in-law see him often?"

"Once or twice a month . . ."

"In the evening?"

"No. During the afternoon. Generally after six o'clock, when Maître Gaillard came back from the law courts."

"Did you used to go with him?"

She shook her head.

Perhaps it was ridiculous, but the Chief Superintendent had lost his bad-tempered look.

"Can I use the telephone?"

"Would you prefer to go up to the office or to use the booth?"

"I'll use the booth."

As Émile Boulay had done, with the difference that Boulay had started dialing only about ten o'clock in the evening. Through the glass he could see Germaine, the cloakroom girl, who was arranging pink tickets in an old cigar box.

"Hello . . . Is that Maître Gaillard's residence?"

"No, monsieur . . . This is Lecot's, the pharmacy . . ."

"Sorry . . ."

He must have got one figure wrong. He dialed again, more carefully, and heard a bell ringing in the distance. One minute, two minutes went by, and nobody answered.

Three times he dialed the same number, always without success. As he left the booth, he looked around for Ada; finally he found her in the dressing room, where two women were stripping. They took no notice of him and made no attempt to conceal their bare breasts.

"Is Maître Gaillard a bachelor?"

"I don't know. I've never heard anybody mention his wife. Perhaps he has one all the same. I have never been to his house."

A little later, out on the sidewalk, Maigret started questioning Mickey.

"Do you know Jean-Charles Gaillard?"

"The lawyer? I know him by name. It was him that defended Big Lucien, three years ago, and got him acquitted."

"He was also your boss's lawyer."

"That doesn't surprise me . . . they say he's very good."

"Do you know if he's married?"

"I'm sorry, Monsieur Maigret, but people like that aren't in my line, and with the best will in the world I can't tell you anything about them."

The Chief Superintendent went back into the booth and dialed the same number, but without getting through.

Then, on the spur of the moment, he telephoned a lawyer he had known for a good many years, Chavanon, and was lucky enough to find him at home.

"Maigret speaking . . . No, I haven't got a client for you in my office . . . I'm not speaking from the Quai des Orfèvres. I'd like some information . . . do you know Maître Jean-Charles Gaillard?"

"Slightly . . . I see him at the courthouse and once I had occasion to lunch with him . . . but he's much too important a person for a humble worker like myself . . ."

"Married?"

"I think so, yes . . . wait a minute . . . yes, I'm certain he is. Just after the war he married a singer or dancer from the Casino de Paris . . . at least, that's what I've been told . . ."

"You've never seen her? You haven't been to his house?"

"They've never invited me there . . ."

"They aren't divorced? They live together?"

"As far as I know . . ."

"I suppose you don't know if she accompanies him when he has a case in the provinces?"

"You don't normally do that."

"Thank you . . ."

He again phoned Rue La Bruyère, in vain, and the cloakroom girl stared at him with growing curiosity.

Finally he decided to leave the Lotus and, after a little wave to Mickey, went slowly down Rue Pigalle. On Rue La Bruyère he soon singled out a building that looked like an ordinary middle-class house, such as one finds everywhere in the provinces and can still find here and there in certain Paris neighborhoods. There were no lights in any of the windows. A brass plate bore the lawyer's name. He pushed a button just above the plate and a bell rang inside the house.

No sound. He rang twice, three times, but with no more success than when he had telephoned.

For no particular reason he crossed the street to look at the house as a whole.

Just as he raised his head, a curtain moved behind a window on the first floor, which was unlighted, and he could have sworn that for a moment he caught sight of a face.

5

Anyone would have thought that Maigret was playing at being a night-club proprietor and that, in spite of the difference in weight and build, he was doing his best to imitate Émile Boulay. Without hurrying, he strolled through the few streets that constituted the former steward's world and, as the hours went by, these changed in appearance.

First there were the neon signs, which became more numerous, and then there were the uniformed doormen who appeared outside the doors. Not only did the sound of jazz filtering through the night club's doors give a different vibration to the air, but also the passers-by were different and the night taxis began to spill out their passengers, while a new fauna moved back and forth between the light and shade.

Women called out to him. He walked along with his hands behind his back. Had Monsieur Émile walked with his hands behind his back? In any case, he hadn't smoked like the Chief Superintendent. He had sucked peppermints.

Maigret walked down Rue Notre-Dame-de-Lorette as far as the Saint-Trop'. He had known the night club under another name, at a time when most of its clients had been ladies in dinner jackets.

Had Montmartre changed so much? The rhythm of the

orchestras was no longer the same. There was more neon lighting, but the people looked like those he had known before; some of them had simply changed their jobs, like the doorman at the Saint-Trop', who greeted the Chief Superintendent familiarly.

He was a colossus with a white beard, a Russian refugee who for years, in another night club in the district, had sung old ballads of his country, in a fine bass voice, accompanying himself on a balalaika.

"Do you remember last Tuesday evening?"

"I remember all the evenings God has allowed me to live," replied the former general grandiloquently.

"Did your employer come here that evening?"

"About half past nine, with a pretty young lady."

"You mean Ada? He didn't come back alone later on?"

"No, I swear by Saint George that he didn't."

Why by Saint George? Maigret went in, glancing at the bar, and at the tables around which the first customers were sitting bathed in an orange light. The staff must have been told that he was there, for waiters, musicians, and hostesses watched him with curiosity mingled with a certain anxiety.

Had Boulay been in the habit of staying longer? Maigret left again, nodded to Mickey outside the Lotus and to the cloakroom girl inside, and asked her for a token for the telephone.

In the glass booth he dialed the Rue La Bruyère number once more, but in vain.

Then he went into the Train Bleu, which was decorated to look like a Pullman carriage. The orchestra was playing so loud that he beat a retreat, plunged into the quiet and darkness of the other part of Rue Victor-Massé, and came to the Square d'Anvers, where only two cafés were open.

One, the Chope d'Anvers, looked like an old-fashioned brasserie in the provinces. Near the windows, customers were playing cards, and at the back there was a billiard table, around which two men were slowly circling with almost solemn movements.

One of the two was Monsieur Raison, in his shirt sleeves. His partner, a man with a huge belly and a cigar between his teeth, was wearing green suspenders.

Maigret did not go in, but stood there for a moment, as if fascinated by the sight, though in fact he was thinking of something else. He started when a voice near him said:

"Good evening, Chief."

It was Lapointe, whom he had told to check up on the accountant, and who explained:

"I was just going home. . . . I've found out how he spent Tuesday evening. He left the café at a quarter past eleven . . . he never stays after half past eleven. . . . Less than ten minutes later he was home.

"The concierge is absolutely definite. She hadn't gone to bed, because that evening her husband and her daughter had gone to the movies and she waited up for them.

"She saw Monsieur Raison come in and she's certain that he didn't go out again."

Young Lapointe was puzzled, for Maigret didn't seem to be listening to him.

"Have you found anything new?" he ventured. "Do you want me to stay with you?"

"No. Go to bed . . ."

He preferred to be alone to start his round again. It was not long before he returned to the Train Bleu, or, to be more precise, opened the curtain and glanced inside, like certain customers who make sure, before going in, that they have found what they are looking for.

Then the Lotus again. Another wink from Mickey, who was engaged in a mysterious conversation with two Americans, to whom he was obviously promising extraordinary amusements.

Maigret did not need to ask for a token for the telephone, and the bell rang yet again in the house whose façade he now knew and where he was convinced that a curtain had moved.

He gave a start when a man's voice said:

"Hello . . ."

He had no longer been expecting a reply.

"Maître Jean-Charles Gaillard?"

"Speaking . . . Who's that?"

"Chief Superintendent Maigret of Police Headquarters."

A pause. Then the voice, rather impatiently, said:

"Yes, all right, go on."

"I must apologize for bothering you at this time of night . . ."

"It's a miracle that you found me in . . . I've just come back from Poitiers by car and I was glancing through my mail before going to bed."

"Could I come and see you for a few minutes?"

"Are you telephoning from the Quai des Orfèvres?"

"No . . . I'm practically next door . . ."

"Right . . . I'll be expecting you . . ."

Mickey still outside the door, the street getting noisier and noisier, and a woman who emerged from a corner and put her hand on the Chief Superintendent's arm drawing back suddenly when she recognized him.

"I'm sorry," she stammered.

He returned, as to an oasis, to the peaceful atmosphere of Rue La Bruyère, where, outside the lawyer's house, a big pastel-blue American car was standing. There was a light above the door. Maigret went up the three steps from the sidewalk; before he could press the electric bell, the door opened into a hall paved with white tiles.

Jean-Charles Gaillard was as tall and broad-shouldered

as the Russian doorman at the Saint-Trop'. He was a man of about forty-five, with a florid complexion and a football player's build, who must have been all muscle at one time, and was only just beginning to put on flesh.

"Come in, Chief Superintendent . . ."

He closed the door, and led his guest to the end of the hallway, where he showed him into his study. The room, which was fairly big and comfortably furnished, but without ostentatious luxury, was lighted only by a lamp with a green shade standing on a desk partly covered with letters that had just been opened.

"Please sit down . . . I've had a tiring day, and on the way back I ran into a heavy storm that held me up . . ."

Maigret was fascinated by the lawyer's left hand, from which four fingers were missing. Only the thumb was left.

"I should like to ask you two or three questions about one of your clients . . ."

Was the lawyer uneasy? Or just curious? It was hard to say. He had blue eyes, and fair hair cropped short.

"If professional secrecy allows me to reply, . . ." he murmured with a smile.

He had finally sat down opposite the Chief Superintendent, and his right hand was toying with an ivory paper-knife.

"Boulay's body was found this morning . . ."

"Boulay?" echoed the other man, as if he were searching his memory.

"The proprietor of the Lotus and three other night clubs . . ."

"Ah, yes . . . I see . . ."

"He came to see you recently, didn't he?"

"That depends on what you mean by recently . . ."

"Tuesday, for example . . ."

"Tuesday this week?"

"Yes."

Jean-Charles Gaillard shook his head.

"If he came I didn't see him. He may have called while I was at the courthouse . . . I shall have to ask my secretary tomorrow . . ."

Looking Maigret in the eye, he asked a question in his turn.

"You say that his body has been found. The fact that you are here suggests that the police are looking into the matter. Am I to understand that it was not a case of natural death?"

"He was murdered . . ."

"That's odd . . ."

"Why?"

"Because, in spite of his profession, he was a decent fellow and I didn't think he had any enemies. It's true that he was just one of many clients . . ."

"When was the last time you saw him?"

"I should be able to give you a definite reply to that. . . . Just a moment . . ."

He got up and went into the adjoining office, where he turned on the lamps and rummaged around in a drawer, coming back with a red notebook.

"My secretary keeps note of all my appointments . . . Wait a moment . . ."

He turned the pages, starting at the back, silently mouthing names. He went through about twenty pages like that.

"Here we are! . . . May 22 at five o'clock. . . . There's a mention of another call on May 18 at eleven o'clock in the morning . . ."

"You haven't seen him since May 22?"

"Not as far as I can remember . . ."

"And he hasn't telephoned you?"

"If he called my office, he would have had my secretary on the line and she will be able to answer your question. She'll be here tomorrow at nine o'clock."

"Did you look after all Boulay's affairs?"

"That depends on what you mean by all his affairs . . ."

He added with a smile:

"That's a dangerous question you've just asked me. I don't necessarily know about all his activities."

"I gather it was you who prepared his income tax return . . ."

"I can see no harm in replying to that question. That's correct. Boulay had very little education and would have been incapable of dealing with it himself . . ."

Another pause, after which he went on:

"I must add that he never asked me to cheat. . . . Naturally, like everybody else, he wanted to pay as little tax as possible, but keeping on the right side of the law. Otherwise I would not have taken on his affairs . . ."

"You mentioned a call he paid you on May 18. . . . The previous night, a certain Mazotti had been killed not far from the Lotus . . ."

Very calm, Gaillard lighted a cigarette, held out the silver box to Maigret, and took it back when he noticed that he was smoking his pipe.

"I can see no harm in telling you why he came. Mazotti had tried the protection trick on him, and, to get rid of him, Boulay had provided himself with the assistance of three or four toughs from his native town of Le Havre . . ."

"I know . . ."

"When he heard about Mazotti's death, he guessed that the police would want to question him. He had nothing to hide, but he was afraid of seeing his name in the papers."

"He asked your advice?"

"Precisely. I told him to reply frankly. I believe, incidentally, that that advice stood him in good stead. Unless I'm mistaken, he was summoned a second time to the Quai des Orfèvres, on the twenty-second or the twenty-third, and he came to see me again before that interview . . . I don't suppose he was ever suspected? In my opinion, that would have been a mistake . . ."

"You are sure that he didn't come back this week? On Tuesday, for example?"

"Not only am I sure that he didn't, but, once again, the appointment, if there had been an appointment, would be recorded in this notebook. See for yourself . . ."

He held it out to the Chief Superintendent, who did not touch it.

"Were you at home on Tuesday night?"

This time the lawyer frowned.

"This is beginning to resemble an interrogation," he observed. "And I must admit that I should like to know what you have in mind . . ."

All the same, he ended up by shrugging his shoulders and smiling.

"If I search my memory, I shall probably be able to tell you how I spent my time . . . I pass most of my evenings in this study, because it is the only time I can work in peace. In the morning, I have a continuous stream of clients. In the afternoon I am usually at the courthouse . . ."

"You didn't dine out?"

"I scarcely ever dine out. . . . You see, I'm not a society lawyer."

"On Tuesday evening then?"

"Today is Friday, isn't it? . . . Saturday, in fact, since it is after midnight. . . . This morning I left very early for Poitiers . . ."

"By yourself?"

The question seemed to surprise him.

"By myself, of course, since I was going there for a

case. Yesterday, I didn't leave my office all evening . . .
Tell me, is it an alibi you want?"

His voice was still amused and ironical.

"What intrigues me is that this alibi has to be for
Tuesday evening, whereas my client's death, if I have
understood you correctly, was quite recent. Still . . . I am
like poor Boulay . . . I like to keep on the right side of the
law. . . . On Thursday, I didn't go out . . . On Wednesday
evening . . . let's see . . on Wednesday I worked until ten
o'clock, and then, as I had a slight headache, I went for a
walk. As for Tuesday . . . I was in court during the afternoon. A complicated case that has been dragging on for
three years, and is far from being over . . . I came home for
dinner . . ."

"You had dinner with your wife?"

Gaillard's gaze rested on the Chief Superintendent and
he said:

"With my wife, yes . . ."

"She is here?"

"She is upstairs . . ."

"Did she go out that night?"

"She hardly ever goes out, because of her health. . . . My
wife has been ill for several years and suffers a great
deal . . ."

"I'm sorry . . ."

"That's all right. . . . As I was saying, we had dinner.
I came downstairs to this study, as usual . . . Ah! . . . Now
I remember . . . I felt tired after my afternoon at the
courthouse. I took my car with the idea of driving for an
hour or two to relax, as I sometimes do . . . I used to play
games a great deal and I miss the fresh air. As I was
driving along the Champs-Élysées, I saw that they were
showing a Russian film I had heard people speak well
of . . ."

"In short, you went to the movies . . ."

"Precisely. As you can see, there was no mystery about it. Afterward I dropped into Fouquet's for a drink before going home."

"Nobody was waiting for you?"

"Nobody."

"You didn't receive a telephone call?"

He seemed to search his memory again.

"I don't think so, no. I must have smoked a cigarette before going up to bed . . . I find it difficult to drop off to sleep. And now allow me to say that I'm rather surprised . . ."

It was Maigret's turn to play the innocent.

"Why?"

"I was expecting you to question me about my client, but you've asked me about myself and about the way I spent my time. I could easily take offense at that . . ."

"The fact is, I'm trying to reconstruct Emile Boulay's movements.

"I don't understand . . ."

"He wasn't killed last night, but Tuesday night . . ."

"But you told me . . ."

"I told you that he was found this morning . . ."

"You mean that, since Tuesday, his body . . ."

Maigret nodded. He looked benign and seemed ready to impart secrets.

"It has been practically established that on Tuesday evening Boulay had an appointment . . . probably an appointment in this neighborhood."

"And you thought that he came here?"

The Chief Superintendent laughed.

"I'm not accusing you of having strangled your client . . ."

"He was strangled?"

"According to the post-mortem. It would take too long to tell you what clues we have collected. He was in the habit of coming to ask your advice . . ."

"I wouldn't have received him at midnight."

"He might have found himself in a tricky situation . . . if, say, someone had tried to blackmail him . . ."

Gaillard lighted another cigarette and slowly blew the smoke out in front of him.

"His checkbook shows that not long ago he drew a fairly large sum out of the bank . . ."

"May I ask you how much?"

"Five thousand francs. That wasn't something he normally did. . . . Usually he took the ready cash he needed out of the till of one of his night clubs . . ."

"Did that happen only once?"

"Only once, as far as we know. I shall know for certain tomorrow, when I check on his account."

"I still can't see where I come into this case . . ."

"I'm coming to that . . .

"Let's suppose that he had given in the first time and that the blackmailer had returned to the attack, making an appointment with him for Tuesday night. . . . The idea might have occurred to him to ask your advice. He would have dialed your number several times during the evening while you were at the movies . . . Who answers the telephone the evenings when you are out?"

"Nobody."

And, as Maigret looked surprised, he went on:

"My wife, as I have already said, is ill. It all began with a nervous breakdown, which has got steadily worse. What's more, she suffers from polyneuritis, which the doctors can't manage to cure. She hardly ever leaves the first floor and there is always a maid with her, who is really a nurse. My wife doesn't know that. I have cut off the telephone upstairs . . ."

"And what about the servants?"

"There are two of them and they sleep on the second floor. . . . To return to your question, which I understand better now, I don't know of any attempt to blackmail my client. I must add that the existence of any blackmail of that sort would surprise me, because, knowing his affairs, I can't see any grounds on which he could have been blackmailed. So he didn't come to ask my advice on Tuesday night. . . . And, a priori, I don't know how he spent the night . . .

"The fact that he had been killed didn't surprise me very much when you told me, because you don't reach the situation he occupied in that world without making some serious enemies. The fact that he had been strangled I find more disturbing . . . and, even more so, the fact that his body wasn't found until this morning . . .

"As a matter of interest, where was it found? . . . I suppose it was fished out of the Seine?"

"It was lying on the sidewalk alongside the Père Lachaise cemetery . . ."

"How did his wife take the news?"

"You know her?"

"I have seen her once. Boulay was mad about her. He insisted on introducing me to her and his children. He invited me to dinner on Rue Victor-Massé and that's how I met the whole family."

"Including Antonio?"

"Including the brother-in-law and his wife . . . a real family gathering. At bottom Boulay was very much a bourgeois, and seeing him at home, you would never have suspected that he lived by undressing women . . ."

"Do you know his night clubs?"

"I went to the Lotus two or three times, over a year ago . . . I also attended the opening of the night club on Rue de Berri . . ."

Maigret was asking himself a lot of questions, without venturing to voice them. Living with a sick wife, didn't the lawyer look elsewhere for the pleasures he no longer found at home?

"Have you met Ada?"

"The young sister? Oh, yes! She was at the dinner party. She's a delightful girl, just as pretty as Marina, but with more of a head on her shoulders."

"Do you think she was her brother-in-law's mistress?"

"I am putting myself in your place, Chief Superintendent. I realize that you have to look in all directions. ... All the same, some of your theories are absolutely fantastic. If you had known Boulay, you wouldn't ask me that question. He hated complications. An affair with Ada would have made an enemy of Antonio, who, as a good Italian, has a highly developed sense of family. Forgive my yawning, but I got up before dawn to arrive in time for my case ..."

"Are you in the habit of leaving your car in front of the house?"

"As a rule, I don't bother to take it to the garage. There's nearly always room ..."

"Forgive me for having bothered you like this. One last question. Did Boulay leave a will?"

"Not to my knowledge. And I can't see why he should have made one. He has two children. What's more, he married under the joint estate system. The inheritance presents no problems at all ..."

"Thank you ..."

"Tomorrow morning I shall go to express my sympathy to his widow and place myself at her disposal. Poor woman!"

There were so many other questions that Maigret would have liked to ask him. For example, how he had come to lose four fingers of his left hand. And also at what time he had left Rue La Bruyère that morning . . . Finally, on account of something Mickey had said, he would have been interested to consult the list of the lawyer's clients.

A few minutes later, he took a taxi on Place Saint-Georges and went home to bed. All the same, he got up at eight o'clock in the morning, and at half past nine he was leaving the office of the Director of Police Headquarters, where he had sat through the morning conference without opening his mouth.

The first thing he did after opening the window and taking off his jacket was to ring up Maître Chavanon, to whom he had telephoned the day before.

"It's me again . . . Maigret. Am I disturbing you?"

"I've got somebody with me . . ."

"Just a piece of information . . . Do you know a colleague of yours who is on fairly friendly terms with Jean-Charles Gaillard?"

"Again! Anybody would think you had a grudge against him . . ."

"No, I haven't got a grudge against him, but I'd like to know a few things that concern him . . ."

"Why not ask the man himself? Go and see him . . ."

"I have seen him."

"Well, then? Was he unco-operative?"

"On the contrary. The fact remains that there are certain questions which are too delicate to ask straight out . . ."

Chavanon was anything but enthusiastic. Maigret had expected this. In almost all professions there exists an *esprit de corps*. You can speak freely about one another among yourselves, but you don't appreciate any form of intrusion. Least of all by the police!

"Listen . . . I've told you all I know . . . I don't know who his friends are at the moment, but a few years ago he was very friendly with Ramuel."

"The fellow who defended the butcher on Rue Caulaincourt?"

"That's the man. I'd be grateful, if you go to see him, if you wouldn't bring me into it. All the more so since he's just obtained two or three acquittals one after the other and it's rather gone to his head. . . . Good luck!"

Maître Ramuel lived on Rue du Bac, and the next moment Maigret had his secretary on the line.

"It's practically impossible. . . . His whole morning is taken . . . Wait a moment . . . If you come about ten to eleven and he has finished quickly with the client he's seeing at half past ten . . ."

They obviously trooped in and out of his rooms like the patients at a local dentist's. Next, please!

Maigret went to Rue du Bac all the same, and, as he was early, he dropped in at the café for a glass of white wine. The walls of the waiting room at Maître Ramuel's were covered with pictures dedicated by the artists. Three people were waiting there, including an old woman who must have been a rich farmer's wife from the country.

Nonetheless, at five to eleven the secretary opened the door and discreetly motioned to the Chief Superintendent to follow her.

Though still young and baby-faced, Maître Ramuel was already bald. He came forward, holding his hand out in a cordial welcome.

"To what do I owe this honor?"

The room was huge, the walls paneled, the furniture Renaissance pieces, and the floor covered with genuine Oriental carpets.

"Sit down. A cigar? . . . Oh, of course not . . . Do smoke your pipe, please . . ."

You could tell that he was bursting with self-importance, he sat down at his desk like an attorney general in the ministerial seat.

"I can't see that any of the cases I have in hand . . ."

"I haven't come about one of your clients, Maître. . . . What's more, I feel rather embarrassed. I should like you to regard my call as a private visit . . ."

Ramuel was so used to trial courts that in his private life he went on behaving as if he were in court, with the same gestures and the same arm movements, from which nothing was lacking but the full sleeves of a black gown.

He began by opening his eyes wide in a comical look, and then spread his hands out to express surprise.

"Come now, Chief Superintendent, you aren't going to tell me you're in trouble? . . . The idea of acting as counsel for Chief Superintendent Maigret . . ."

"I just need a little information about somebody . . ."

"One of my clients?"

He assumed an indignant expression.

"I don't need to remind you . . ."

"Have no fear. I'm not asking you to break your oath of professional secrecy. For reasons which it would take too long to explain, I need to know something about one of your colleagues . . ."

The brows furrowed, again in an exaggerated way, as if the lawyer were acting his usual comedy before a jury.

"I'm not asking you to betray a friendship either . . ."

"Go on. I make no promises, you understand . . ."

It was annoying, but the Chief Superintendent had no choice.

"I believe you know your colleague Jean-Charles Gaillard quite well . . ."

An air of false embarrassment.

"We used to see a lot of each other . . ."

"You have quarreled?"

"Let us say that we meet less frequently than before . . ."

"Do you know his wife?"

"Jeanine? I met her for the first time when she was still

dancing at the Casino de Paris . . . that was just after the war. A delightful girl at that time . . . and beautiful! They called her the beautiful Lara and people used to turn around to look at her in the street."

"Was that her name?"

"No. Her real name was Dupin, but as a dancer she used the name of Jeanine de Lara. She would probably have had a brilliant career . . ."

"She gave it up for Gaillard?"

"When he married her, he promised that he wouldn't ask her to leave the stage."

"And he didn't keep his word?"

What followed now was a comedy of discretion. Ramuel seemed to weigh the pros and cons, and heaved a sigh, as if he were being torn by contrary feelings.

"After all, everybody in Paris society knows all about it . . . Gaillard had just come back from the war, covered with medals . . ."

"It was in the war that he lost four fingers?"

"Yes. He was at Dunkirk. In England he joined the Free French forces. He went through the African campaign, and then, unless I'm mistaken, found himself in Syria. He was a lieutenant in the Commandos. He never talks about it, I must admit. He isn't the kind of person that likes talking about his wartime exploits. One night when he was supposed to be taking an enemy patrol by surprise, it was he who was surprised, and he only saved his life by grabbing hold of the knife that was being plunged into his chest. He's a tough character.

"He fell madly in love with Jeanine and decided to marry her. At that time he was working under Maître Jouane, the common lawyer, and wasn't making much. . . .

"He was a jealous man, and spent his evenings in the wings of the Casino de Paris. . . .

"You can guess the rest. Little by little he persuaded

his wife to give up dancing. He started working extremely hard to keep the pot boiling . . . I often sent him clients . . ."

"He's always stuck to common law?"

This time Ramuel assumed the embarrassed expression of a man wondering whether his interlocutor will be capable of understanding him.

"It's rather complicated. There are some lawyers you rarely see at the law courts but who have an important clientele all the same. . . . They are the ones who earn the most money . . . they are legal advisers to big companies. They know company law inside out, and its subtlest points . . ."

"Is that the case with Gaillard?"

"Yes and no. Mind you, I haven't seen him for several years . . . he doesn't often appear in court. . . . As for his clientele, I should find it hard to describe. Unlike his former chief, he doesn't have big banks and industrial firms among his clients . . ."

Maigret listened patiently, trying to guess at what lay behind the words.

"With the present fiscal laws, a lot of people need professional advice. Some people, because of the nature of their work, need to make sure that they are keeping on the right side of the law . . ."

"The proprietor of a chain of night clubs, for instance?"

Ramuel made a show of surprise and confusion.

"I didn't know I had been so explicit . . . Mind you, I don't know whom you're talking about."

Maigret remembered his conversation the previous day with Louis Boubée, alias Mickey. Both of them had recalled the days of the Tivoli and La Tétoune, at whose restaurant you used to meet not only the big bosses of the underworld, but their lawyers and a certain number of politicians.

"Boulay has been killed," he said abruptly.

"Boulay?"

"Monsieur Émile . . . the owner of the Lotus, the Train Bleu, and two other night clubs . . ."

"I haven't had time to read the paper this morning . . . Was he a client of Gaillard's?"

He was disarming in his naïveté.

"Obviously that's one of the categories I was talking about. It isn't easy, in certain professions, to avoid trouble. . . . What happened to this man Boulay?"

"He has been strangled . . ."

"How horrible!"

"You were talking just now about Madame Gaillard . . ."

"It seems that her condition has deteriorated since I lost sight of her. . . . It began, at the time when I was still friendly with them, with nervous breakdowns, which became increasingly frequent. I suppose that she couldn't get used to middle-class life. Let's see . . . how old is she now? . . . In her forties, unless I'm mistaken. She must be four or five years younger than he is . . . but she has gone to pieces. . . . She has aged very quickly.

"Without being a doctor, Chief Superintendent, I've seen quite a few women, especially among the most beautiful ones, take that bend rather badly. . . .

"I've heard people say that she is practically insane, that she sometimes spends weeks at a time in a darkened room. . . .

"I'm sorry for Gaillard. He's an intelligent fellow, one of the most intelligent I know. He worked like a dog to get ahead in the world . . . He tried to give Jeanine a brilliant social life . . . because for a while they lived very well indeed. . . .

"But all that wasn't enough. And now . . ."

If his face expressed compassion, there nonetheless remained a gleeful, ironical flicker in his little eyes.

"What was it that you wanted to know? . . . Mind you, I haven't told you anything confidential . . . you could have questioned anybody at the law courts."

"I suppose Jean-Charles Gaillard has never had any trouble with the Bar Association?"

This time Ramuel spread out his arms and looked shocked.

"Come, come! What are you suggesting?"

He stood up and glanced at the clock on the mantelpiece.

"I'm sorry, but you probably saw that a certain number of clients are waiting for me . . . I've got a case at two . . . I presume that nobody knows about your visit and that what we have said remains between ourselves?"

And, going toward the door with a skipping step, he sighed theatrically:

"Poor Jeanine!"

6

Before going home for lunch, Maigret had dropped in at the Quai des Orfèvres, and had said to Lapointe, almost absent-mindedly:

"I should like you to go and scout around Rue La Bruyère and the surrounding area as soon as possible. It seems that a pale-blue American car is usually parked, day and night, outside Maître Jean-Charles Gaillard's private house..."

He handed him a piece of paper on which he had scribbled the car's registration number.

"I should like to know at what time the car was there on Tuesday evening, and also at what time it left yesterday morning or during the night..."

Maigret had the wide-eyed, vacant look, the hunched shoulders, and the slow, deliberate gait typical of him at certain times.

At those times, people who saw him—his colleagues more than anyone else—imagined that he was concentrating. In fact, nothing could have been further from the truth. But no matter how often he told them this, they refused to believe him.

What he was really doing was rather ridiculous, not to say childish. He took an idea, a phrase, and repeated it to himself like a schoolboy trying to memorize a lesson. Sometimes he would even start moving his lips and talking under his breath alone in the middle of his office, in the street, anywhere.

The words did not necessarily mean anything. Sometimes they sounded like a joke.

"There have been cases of a lawyer being killed by his client, but I've never heard of a client being killed by his lawyer..."

That did not mean that he was accusing Jean-Charles Gaillard of having strangled the puny proprietor of the Lotus and the other night clubs. His wife would have surprised him if, while he was eating, she had suddenly asked him:

"What are you thinking about?"

He would probably have replied in good faith that he was not thinking about anything. There were also pictures that he kept passing through his head as if through a magic lantern.

Émile Boulay, in the evening, standing on the sidewalk outside the Lotus, virtually a nightly habit . . . The little man looking at the sky, at the crowd flowing by, which changed in rhythm and almost in nature as the evening wore on, and calculating the receipts in his four night clubs . . .

The second picture was not an everyday one. Boulay went into the booth, under the eyes of the cloakroom girl, and dialed a number that did not answer . . .

Three times . . . four times. Between calls he went for a little walk, either inside the club or out in the street. . . . And it was only at the fifth or sixth attempt that he finally succeeded in getting an answer.

But he did not leave immediately. Standing beside Mickey on the sidewalk, he took his watch out of his pocket every now and then . . .

"He didn't go home to get his automatic," Maigret nearly said aloud.

Émile had a license. He was entitled to be armed. At the time when Mazotti and his gang had been bothering him, he had always been armed.

If he was not armed that particular evening, it was because he had no suspicion of danger.

Finally, without saying anything to the doorman who looked like a wizened little boy, he started walking unhurriedly down Rue Pigalle.

That was the last picture. Or at least the last picture of Émile alive.

"Have you any plans for tomorrow?"

He raised his head from over his plate and looked at his wife, as if he were surprised to see her opposite him, near the open window.

"Tomorrow?" he echoed, in a voice so neutral that she burst out laughing.

"You were far away! Forgive me for . . ."

"What's tomorrow?"

"It's Sunday . . . Do you think you'll have some work to do?"

He hesitated before replying. He did not know. He had not thought about Sunday. He hated interrupting an investigation, maintaining that one of the principal chances of success lay in speed. The more days that went by, the more difficult it was to obtain clear evidence from witnesses. He himself felt the need to keep going, to stay with the little society into which he had been plunged.

And now here was a Sunday, in other words a hole. And the afternoon, too, was going to be practically wasted, because for most people Saturday had become a sort of Sunday.

"I don't know yet . . . I'll phone you in the afternoon..."

Spreading his arms out in the theatrical manner of Maître Ramuel, he added:

"I'm sorry. It isn't my fault . . ."

Naturally, the life at Police Headquarters had already begun slowing down. There were offices that were empty, superintendents and inspectors who had gone off to the country.

"Lapointe isn't back, is he?"

"Not yet, Chief."

He had just caught sight of fat Torrence, in the inspectors' room, who was showing his colleagues a reel for a fishing rod. He could not expect everybody to be hypnotized by Émile Boulay like himself.

He did not know what to do while he was waiting for Lapointe, and he had not the courage, on a Saturday afternoon, to plunge back into his administrative plans.

He ended up by dropping in on Lecoin, his colleague of the Vice Squad, who was reading the paper. Lecoin looked more like a gangster than a detective.

"Am I disturbing you?"

"Not at all."

Maigret went and sat down on the window sill, without quite knowing why he had come.

"Did you know the proprietor of the Lotus?"

"As I know them all . . ."

The conversation, a lazy one without either head or tail, lasted almost an hour without producing any results. According to Lecoin, the former steward was a decent fellow who did not belong to the underworld and whom some people in Montmartre contemptuously called the "Grocer."

By four o'clock, Sunday had almost begun, and the Chief Superintendent once again pushed open the door of the inspectors' room.

"Lapointe?"

"Not back yet, Chief . . ."

He knew that it would not help, but nonetheless he

opened the door leading to the law courts and ambled into the adjoining building. That morning he had decided to go to the registry and obtain a list of the clients whom Jean-Charles Gaillard had represented in court.

The law courts were practically empty, with drafts blowing along the vast corridors, and when he pushed open the door of the registry, he found nobody there. It was curious. Anybody could have gone in and rummaged about in the green filing cabinets that lined the walls up to the ceiling. Anybody, too, could have taken a gown from the attorneys' cloakroom, and even sat in a judge's chair.

"The zoo is better guarded than this," he growled.

At last he found Lapointe in his office.

"I've come back empty-handed, Chief. . . . But I've questioned nearly all the people who live in that street . . . at any rate those who haven't gone off for the weekend.

"The blue American car is familiar to them all. Some of them know whom it belongs to. . . . Others notice it every morning when they set off for work, without bothering their heads about it. When I mentioned Tuesday night to them, most of them shrugged their shoulders hopelessly.

"For them it's a long time ago. Some had already gone to bed at ten o'clock in the evening. . . . Others came back from the movies about half past eleven without paying any attention to the cars, which, at that time of night, are parked all along the street. . . .

"The most common reply was:

"'It's always there . . .'

"They are used to seeing it in its place, you understand, so that even if it isn't there, they think it is . . .

"I went around all the local garages. There's only one where they remember the car and a big, red-faced fellow who sometimes has it filled up there. . . . But he isn't a regular customer. . . .

"There are two garages left where I wasn't able to

question anybody, for the very good reason that they are closed until Monday morning. . . ."

Maigret spread his arms out again like Maître Ramuel. What could he do about it?

"Go back there on Monday," he sighed.

The telephone rang. He recognized Antonio's voice, and hoped for a moment that the Italian had something new to tell him.

"Is that you, Monsieur Maigret? . . . I've got the undertaker's man with me . . . He suggests arranging the funeral for ten o'clock on Monday morning . . . I don't want to give him an answer without your permission. . . ."

What did that matter to Maigret?

"All right . . ."

"You will be receiving an invitation. The Requiem Mass will be at the Church of Notre-Dame-de-Lorette."

He replaced the receiver and gazed vacantly at Lapointe, who was standing there waiting for instructions.

"You can go now. Have a good Sunday. . . . If Lucas is next door, send him in to me."

Lucas was there.

"Anything new, Chief?"

"Not a thing. . . . I should like you to go to the court registry first thing on Monday morning, and get hold of the list of cases in which Jean-Charles Gaillard has appeared. No need to go back to the year zero . . . just the last two or three years . . ."

"Are you going back to Montmartre tonight?"

He shrugged his shoulders. What was the use? He repeated to Lucas what he had already said to Lapointe:

"Have a good Sunday . . ."

And he picked up the receiver.

"Get me my home number. Hello . . . Is that you? . . ."

As if he didn't know that it couldn't be anyone else and as if he didn't recognize her voice!

"Do you remember the train schedule for Morsang? . . .
Today, yes. Before dinner if possible . . . Five fifty-two? . . .
Would you like to spend tonight and tomorrow there? . . .
Good! . . . Get the little suitcase ready . . . No . . . I'll phone
them myself. . . ."

It was on the banks of the Seine, a few miles upstream
from Corbeil. There was an old inn there, the Vieux
Garçon, where, for over twenty years, the Maigrets had
sometimes gone to spend Sunday.

Maigret had discovered it in the course of an investigation, standing all by itself on the riverbank. It was
mainly frequented by anglers.

By now the two of them were well known there. They
were nearly always given the same room, and the same
table under the trees on the terrace for dinner and lunch.

"Hello . . . Get me the Vieux Garçon at Morsang . . .
near Corbeil . . . The Vieux Garçon, yes . . . it's an inn . . ."

Looking through some old books, he had discovered
that the place had been frequented in the past by Balzac
and Alexandre Dumas, and that, later on, literary luncheon
parties had brought together there the Goncourt brothers,
Flaubert, Zola, Alphonse Daudet, and a few others.

"Hello . . . Maigret speaking . . . What's that? . . . Yes,
it's a lovely day . . ."

He knew that as well as the *patronne*.

"Our room is taken? . . . You've got another, but it
doesn't look out on the Seine? . . . That doesn't matter.
We'll arrive in time for dinner."

So, after all, in spite of Émile Boulay, they went and
spent a quiet Sunday by the river. The clientele of the
Vieux Garçon had changed over the years. The anglers
Maigret had met in the old days had nearly all disappeared. Either they were dead, or they had grown too old
to move around.

New anglers had taken their places. They were just as

fanatical as their predecessors; some of them baited their hook several days in advance.

They used to hear some who got up at four o'clock in the morning to go and moor their boat in the current between a couple of stakes.

There was a new, younger crowd consisting mainly of couples who owned small sailboats, and these people danced on the terrace to music from a record player until one o'clock in the morning.

Maigret slept all the same, heard some cocks crowing, the footsteps of the anglers going fishing, and finally got up at nine o'clock.

About ten o'clock, as they were finishing their breakfast under the trees and watching the sails go by, Madame Maigret asked:

"Aren't you going to do any fishing?"

He had neither his fishing rods nor his tackle with him, having left them in their little house at Meung-sur-Loire, but he could always borrow some from the *patronne*.

Why should a lawyer kill his client? You sometimes heard of a patient killing his doctor, out of a conviction that he had been given the wrong treatment. The opposite was extremely rare. The only case he could remember was that of Bougrat.

Émile Boulay was not the aggressive type. He could not claim that his lawyer had let him down, since he had never been convicted and his record was clean.

"Pick any rod you like. The lines are in the cupboard, and you'll find some maggots in the usual place."

They followed the bank, one behind the other, and picked a shady spot near a dead tree. Fate willed it that after half an hour Maigret had already caught a dozen roach. If he had provided himself with a spoon net, he would probably have also landed the chub that weighed over a pound and broke his line.

It is true that after that he did not get another bite. His wife read a magazine, breaking off every now and then to look at him with an amused smile.

They lunched in their corner, with, as usual, people turning to look at them and starting to whisper. Isn't the Chief of the Crime Squad entitled to spend a Sunday in the country like anybody else and go fishing if he feels like it?

He returned to the riverbank, but caught nothing more, and at six o'clock in the evening he and his wife were in the crowded train traveling to Paris.

They had some cold meat and watched the darkness fall, the streets, which were still practically empty, and the houses across the way, where a few lights were beginning to go on.

Boulay did not use to spend his Sundays in the country. His night clubs were open seven days a week, and he was not the man to leave them without supervision. As for his three women, they probably felt no desire to leave their little Italy on Rue Victor-Massé.

At nine o'clock on Monday morning Maigret looked in at the Quai des Orfèvres to make sure that there was nothing new, and at a quarter to ten a taxi deposited him on Rue Pigalle. A funeral notice with a black border was fastened to the grille of the Lotus. On Rue Victor-Massé, there was another on the door of the Train Bleu.

The sidewalk across from what had been Boulay's home was swarming with people. Every now and then, somebody or some small group broke away to go into the house, whose door was hung with black draperies.

Like the others, he waited his turn in front of the elevator, where you got an advance whiff of the flowers and tapers. The living room had been transformed into a mortuary chapel, and some dark figures were standing around the coffin—Antonio, Monsieur Raison, and an old headwaiter who was regarded as one of the family—while a woman could be heard sobbing in a nearby room.

He shook hands, went downstairs again, and waited with the others. He recognized faces he had glimpsed in the dead man's night clubs. All his staff must have been there; the women in fantastically high heels had tired faces, eyes that looked surprised to see the morning sun.

"Quite a crowd, eh?"

It was the doorman, Louis Boubée, alias Mickey, dressed in black, who had tugged the Chief Superintendent by the sleeve and seemed proud of the success the funeral was having.

"They're all here . . ."

He meant the proprietors of all the night clubs in Paris, including those on the Champs-Élysées and in Montparnasse, the musicians, the barmen, the waiters . . .

"Have you seen Jo?"

He pointed to Jo the Wrestler, who waved to the Chief Superintendent and who was also dressed in black for the occasion.

"A mixed crowd, isn't it?"

Loud suits, light-colored hats, big signet rings, and shoes in suède or crocodile. Everybody had come. Boulay might not have belonged to the underworld and might have deserved the nickname of the "Grocer," but he still had been part of the night life of Montmartre.

"You don't know who did it yet?"

At that moment the lawyer came out of the house, which the Chief Superintendent had not seen him enter; the hearse, which had just drawn up alongside the sidewalk, hid him from Maigret almost immediately.

There were so many flowers and wreaths that they filled two whole cars. Behind the hearse, Antonio walked by himself, followed by the staff and the dancers. Then came all the other mourners, forming a procession over a hundred yards long.

The shopkeepers on the way came out to watch, housewives stopped on the curb, and people leaned out of windows. Finally, running alongside the dark line of people, there were photographers taking shots of the procession.

The organ boomed out just as the six men carrying the coffin crossed the threshold of the church. The women followed, wearing thick veils. For a moment, Jean-Charles Gaillard's eyes met those of the Chief Superintendent; then the two men were separated by the crowd.

Maigret stayed at the back of the church, into which a ray of sunshine penetrated every time the door opened. And he went on passing the same pictures through his head, like a pack of cards.

Boulay taking his watch out of his pocket . . . Boulay waiting for a few minutes before walking down the Rue Pigalle . . .

Antonio had done things handsomely. There was not just a funeral service but a sung Mass.

The congregation took a long time coming out. Four or five cars were waiting for the family and the dead man's closest colleagues, for there was no room left in the Montmartre cemetery and Boulay's body was destined for Ivry.

Antonio found time to make his way through the crowd to reach the Chief Superintendent.

"Would you like a place in one of the cars?"

Maigret shook his head. He was watching the lawyer walking away and he elbowed his way after him.

"A fine funeral," he observed, rather as Mickey had said on Rue Victor-Massé. "You're not going to the cemetery?"

"I've got some work waiting for me. Besides, I wasn't invited . . ."

"The whole of Montmartre was there . . ."

Some of the crowd was still drifting away when the hearse and the other cars drove off.

"You must have recognized quite a few of your clients."

"So would any other lawyer."

Changing the subject, as if he found that one distasteful, Gaillard asked:

"Have you got a line on the murderer?"

"Let's call it the beginning of a line . . ."

"What do you mean?"

"I still haven't got the main thing, namely the motive . . ."

"You've got all the rest?"

"I haven't any proof yet, I'm afraid . . . Did you go to the country yesterday?"

The lawyer looked at him in surprise.

"Why do you ask that?"

They, like many other people, were walking up Rue Notre-Dame-de-Lorette, which had rarely been so crowded at that hour of the day, and were just passing the Saint-Trop'; the frame containing the photographs of naked women had been removed and the funeral notice put in its place.

"No reason in particular," replied Maigret. "Because I went there with my wife . . . Because most Parisians, on Sunday, go to the country or to the seaside . . ."

"My wife hasn't been able to go away for a long time now . . ."

"So that you spend Sunday by yourself on Rue La Bruyère?"

"I take the opportunity to study my files."

Was Jean-Charles Gaillard wondering why the Chief Superintendent was keeping close to him? Normally Maigret would have gone down toward the center of the city. But he continued to keep in step with the lawyer, and soon they found themselves on Rue La Bruyère, where the blue car was in its place in front of the house.

There was a moment of embarrassment. Maigret showed no sign of going away. The lawyer was holding his key.

"I won't ask you in, because I know how busy you are..."

"As it happens, I was just going to ask you if I might use your telephone ..."

The door opened.

"Come into my study ..."

The door leading into the adjoining office was open and a secretary about thirty years old stood up. Without taking any notice of Maigret, she spoke to her employer.

"There have been two calls, one of them from Cannes ..."

"I'll see about them later, Lucette ..."

Gaillard seemed preoccupied.

"Is it a local call you want to make? Here's the telephone."

"Thank you ..."

Through the window he could see a paved courtyard in the middle of which there was a rather fine linden tree.

Still standing, Maigret dialed his number.

"Hello ... Has Inspector Lapointe got back? ... Put me through to him, will you? ... Thank you ... Yes ... Hello ... Lapointe? ... Did you find what you were looking for?"

He listened for a long time, while the lawyer, without sitting down at his desk, moved some files around.

"Yes ... yes ... I see ... You're sure about the dates ... You got him to sign a statement? ... No, I'm on Rue La Bruyère. Is Lucas back? ... Not yet? ..."

While he was talking, he looked at the courtyard, at a couple of blackbirds hopping about on the paving stones, at the shadow of the lawyer as he walked up and down in front of the window.

"Yes, wait for me. I won't be long and there may be something new . . ."

He, too, was entitled to play his little comedy. After replacing the receiver, he mimed embarrassment, scratching his head with a perplexed expression.

The two of them were still standing, and the lawyer was looking at him inquisitively. Maigret prolonged the silence on purpose. When he spoke, it was to say, with a hint of reproach in his voice:

"You haven't a very good memory, Monsieur Gaillard . . ."

"What are you insinuating?"

"Or else, for some reason I can't quite fathom, you haven't been telling me the truth . . ."

"What about?"

"Don't you know?"

"I swear I . . ."

He was a tall, strong man, who only a few moments before had been quite sure of himself. But now his face looked like that of a little boy caught red-handed and insisting on protesting his innocence.

"I honestly don't know what you mean . . ."

"Do you mind if I smoke?"

"Of course not."

Maigret slowly filled his pipe, scowling like a man who has an unpleasant task to perform.

The other man said:

"Won't you sit down?"

"I won't be a moment. . . . When I came to see you on Friday, I spoke to you about your car . . ."

"That's possible. . . . We had a rather disjointed conversation and I was too struck by what I had just learned to register any details . . ."

"You told me that your car was usually parked in front of your house and that you left it there for the night . . ."

"That's correct. . . It spent last night there, for instance, and the night before that. You may have seen it as you came in . . ."

"But recently there were a few days when it wasn't there . . ."

He acted as if he were searching his memory.

"Wait a moment . . ."

He had suddenly gone very red, and Maigret almost felt sorry for him. It was obvious that it was only thanks to a tremendous effort that he retained an air of self-assurance.

"I can't remember whether it was last week or the week before that the car needed some repairs . . . I can ask my secretary. It was she who telephoned to the garage to pick it up . . ."

All the same, he made no move toward the communicating door.

"Call her in . . ."

He finally pushed open the door.

"Will you come in here for a moment? The Chief Superintendent has a question he wants to ask you . . ."

"Don't be alarmed, mademoiselle. It's a very innocent question. I should like to know what day you telephoned to the garage on Rue Ballu to come and get the car . . ."

She looked at her employer as if to ask his permission to reply.

"Monday afternoon," she said at last.

"You mean last Monday?"

"Yes . . ."

She was pretty and pleasant, and her white nylon dress revealed an appetizing body. Was there something between her and Gaillard? . . . That was none of Maigret's business for the moment.

"Was it a big repair job?"

"I can show you the bill from the garage. I received it this morning . . . they had to change the muffler. They had thought they would be able to bring the car back on Wednesday morning . . ."

"And they didn't?"

"They phoned to apologize . . . It's an American car . . . Contrary to their expectations, there wasn't a spare muffler available in Paris and they had to telephone to their depot at Le Havre . . ."

Jean-Charles Gaillard was pretending to have no interest in the conversation and, seated at last at his desk, was looking through a file.

"When was the car delivered?"

"Thursday or Friday . . . Will you excuse me? It's marked in my diary . . ."

She went into her office and came back a moment later.

"Thursday evening. They had the muffler delivered by express and worked all day . . ."

"You didn't come back after dinner?"

Another glance at the lawyer.

"No. That rarely happens . . . only when there is some urgent work to be done."

"That didn't happen last week?"

She shook her head unhesitatingly.

"I haven't worked in the evening for at least two weeks."

"Thank you, mademoiselle."

She went out, closing the door behind her, and Maigret stood there, his pipe in his mouth, in the middle of the study.

"Well, that's that," he muttered in the end.

"What's what?"

"Nothing. A little fact which may be important, just as it may not. You know enough about our work to know that we've no right to neglect anything . . ."

"I don't see what my car . . ."

"If you were in my place, you would see. Thank you for letting me use your telephone. It's time that I went back to the office."

The lawyer stood up.

"You have nothing else to ask me?"

"What would I have to ask you? I put all the questions to you on Friday that I wanted to put to you. I presume you answered me truthfully?"

"I have no reason to . . ."

"Quite. All the same, with regard to your car . . ."

"I admit that I had forgotten all about it. This was the third or fourth time in the last few months that that car needed repairs, and that's why I'm thinking of selling it."

"You used taxis for three days?"

"That's correct . . . I sometimes take taxis even when the car is outside my house. You don't have to look for a place to park."

"I see. Have you got a case this afternoon?"

"No. I've already told you that I don't often appear in court. I am more a legal adviser . . ."

"So you will be at home all afternoon?"

"Unless I have an appointment somewhere else. Just a moment . . ."

He opened the door of the adjoining office again.

"Lucette! Will you look and see if I have an outside appointment this afternoon?"

Maigret had the impression that the young woman had been crying. Neither eyes nor nose was red, but her eyes were troubled and uneasy.

"I don't think so . . . all your appointments are here."

All the same, she consulted the red diary.

"No . . ."

"There's your answer," concluded the lawyer.

"Thank you."

"Do you think you'll need me?"

"I've nothing definite in mind, but one never knows. . . . Good-by, mademoiselle."

She nodded to him without looking at him. As for Jean-Charles Gaillard, he led the Chief Superintendent to the front hall. The door of the waiting room was half open, and as they passed they caught sight of the legs of a man.

"Thank you again for letting me use the telephone . . ."

"Don't mention it . . ."

"And forgive me for bothering you. . . ."

When, after walking about fifty yards along the sidewalk, Maigret turned around, Gaillard was still standing at the door, following him with his eyes.

7

It had happened several times, indeed quite often, but never in such a clear, characteristic way. You work in a given direction all the more stubbornly when you are not too sure of yourself and have little data in hand.

You tell yourself that you remain free, when the time comes, to make a turn and search in another direction.

You send inspectors right and left. You think you are marking time, and then you discover a new clue and you start moving cautiously forward.

And all of a sudden, just when you least expect it, the case slips out of your grasp. You cease to be in control of it. It is events that are in command and that force you to take measures you had not foreseen, and for which you were not prepared.

In these cases there are a few uncomfortable hours to get through. You rack your brains. You ask yourself whether you were headed in the wrong direction from the start, and whether you are not going to find yourself faced with a blank wall or, worse still, with a reality different from what you had imagined.

What, in fact, had been Maigret's sole starting point? A simple conviction, backed up, admittedly, by experience: *members of the underworld do not strangle.* They use a gun and sometimes a knife, but in all the records at

Police Headquarters there was no trace of a single crime by strangulation that could be laid at their door.

A second accepted idea was that they leave their victim where he lies. Again, there was not a single instance in the archives of a criminal having kept a corpse at home for several days before dumping it on a sidewalk.

Thus the Chief Superintendent had been hypnotized by Émile Boulay's last evening, by his telephone calls, by his wait on the sidewalk, beside the uniformed Mickey, until the moment when the former steward had walked slowly away down Rue Pigalle.

The whole edifice of Maigret's thought was built on these foundations and on the story of the five thousand francs withdrawn from the bank on May 22.

It presumed that there was no emotional tangle in the little Italy on Rue Victor-Massé, that the three women got along together as well as they appeared to, that Boulay had no mistress elsewhere, and finally that Antonio was an honest individual.

If a single one of these hypotheses—or, rather, of these convictions—was incorrect, the whole of his case fell to the ground.

Perhaps that was why he kept his bad-tempered look and moved ahead only with a certain repugnance.

It was a hot afternoon; the sun was beating down on the window, so that the Chief Superintendent had lowered the blind. He and Lucas had taken off their jackets, and, behind closed doors, were engaged in a task that would probably have made an examining magistrate shrug his shoulders.

It is true that the magistrate in charge of the case was leaving them in peace, convinced that it was a matter of an unimportant underworld vendetta, and the press was showing no greater interest.

"A lawyer doesn't kill his clients . . ."

This was becoming a refrain that Maigret could not get rid of, any more than he could get rid of a song heard again and again on the radio or television.

"A lawyer . . ."

Yet he had gone that morning, after the funeral, to the house of Maître Jean-Charles Gaillard, though admittedly he had been as cautious as possible. As if by accident, coming out of the church, he had accompanied him as far as Rue La Bruyère, and, while he had asked a few questions, he had taken care not to press him too hard.

"A lawyer doesn't kill . . ."

That was no more certain, and no more logical either, than the other statement he had taken as his starting point.

"Criminals don't strangle . . ."

Only you can't summon a well-known lawyer to the Quai des Orfèvres and submit him to an interrogation lasting several hours without risking having the Bar, if not the whole machinery of the law, after your skin.

Some professions are more sensitive than others. He had noticed this when he had telephoned his friend Chavanon, and then when he had called on the ineffable Maître Ramuel.

"A lawyer doesn't kill his clients . . ."

Now it was Jean-Charles Gaillard's clients that the two men were considering in the aureoled quiet of Maigret's office. Lucas had come back from the registry with a list that a clerk had helped him compile.

And Lucas, too, was beginning to have an idea. It was still very vague. He could not manage to express what he was thinking.

"The clerk said something odd to me . . ."

"What?"

"First of all, when I mentioned the name of Jean-Charles

Gaillard, he gave a peculiar smile. Then I asked him for the list of cases Gaillard had taken on during the last two years and his eyes got even more malicious . . .

" 'You won't find many,' he told me.

" 'Because he hasn't got many clients?'

" 'On the contrary! From all I hear, he has a huge clientele and people say he earns more than certain leading trial lawyers who appear every week at the Assizes . . .' "

Lucas, intrigued, went on:

"I tried to get him to talk, but for a while he rummaged about in his files in silence. Every now and then, noting a name and a date on a piece of paper, he muttered:

" 'An acquittal . . .'

"Then, a little later:

" 'Another acquittal . . .'

"And all the time he had that knowing look of his, which infuriated me.

" 'Well, well! A conviction . . . with suspension of sentence, of course . . .'

"This went on for a quite a while. The list got longer. Acquittal followed acquittal, with an occasional suspension or a light sentence.

"I finally insinuated:

" 'He must be very good . . .'

"Then he looked at me as if he were quietly laughing at me and said:

" 'You might say he knows how to pick his cases. . . .' "

It was that phrase that intrigued Lucas and on which Maigret's brain had started working.

Obviously it was more pleasant, not only for the accused, but for his counsel, to win a case than to lose it. His reputation grew all the time and his clientele increased with each new success.

"To pick his cases . . ."

At the moment, the two men were going through the list Lucas had brought. They had made a preliminary classification. On one sheet of paper, the inspector had noted down the common law cases. As neither of them was familiar with that domain, they decided to leave it aside for the time being.

The other cases turned out to be few in number: thirty or so in two years. Which had enabled Jean-Charles Gaillard to state:

"I don't often appear in court..."

Lucas took the names one by one.

"Hippolyte Tessier ... forgery ... acquitted on September 1..."

Both of them would search their memories. If they found nothing, Maigret would go and open the door of the inspectors' room.

"Tessier ... forgery. Does that mean anything to you?"

"Isn't he the former manager of a casino somewhere in Brittany who tried to start a secret gaming club in Paris?"

They went on to the next case.

"Julien Vendre ... housebreaking ... acquitted ..."

Maigret remembered this man. He was a quiet fellow who looked like a sad little clerk, and who had made a specialty of stealing transistors. He had not been caught red-handed and there was no definite proof against him. The Chief Superintendent had advised the magistrate not to press the charge but to wait for the man to incriminate himself further.

"Put him down on the third sheet. ..."

In the meantime, fat Torrence was installed in the shade of a café opposite the lawyer's house; and a police car with no distinguishing marks was waiting a few yards down the street, not far from the blue American car.

If Torrence had to spend the whole afternoon at his table, watching the door across the street, how many glasses would he drink?

"Urbain Potier . . . receiving . . . one year with suspension of sentence."

It was Lucas who had been in charge of the investigation a few months before, and the man had come several times to the Quai des Orfèvres—an obese individual as unprepossessing as Monsieur Raison, the accountant, with tufts of black hair coming out of his nostrils.

He kept a junk shop on Boulevard de La Chapelle. You could find anything there—old kerosene lamps as well as refrigerators and threadbare clothes.

"I'm an honest shopkeeper . . . poor, but honest. When that fellow came and sold me those lead pipes, I didn't know he'd stolen them. I took him for . . ."

At every name Maigret hesitated. A dozen times the door of the inspectors' room was opened for a question.

"Write . . ."

"Gaston Mauran . . . car theft."

"A little red-haired fellow."

"It doesn't say so on my paper . . ."

"Last spring?"

"Yes . . . in April. He belonged to a gang that repainted cars and sent them into the provinces for resale."

"Call Dupeu . . ."

Inspector Dupeu had been in charge of that case, and, by a stroke of luck, he happened to be in the next room.

"It was a little red-haired fellow, wasn't it, who gave us that story about his old sick mother?"

"Yes, Chief. As a matter of fact, he did have an old sick mother. He was only nineteen at the time. He was the least important member of the gang. He just kept watch while Mad Justin stole the cars."

Two cases of procuring; some more burglaries. Nothing world-shaking. Nothing that had hit the front page of the newspapers.

By contrast, all the lawyer's other clients were more or less professionals.

"Go on," sighed Maigret.

"That's the lot. You told me not to go back further than two years . . ."

There was not enough there to occupy the time of a lawyer who had his own town house in Paris, even if it was only a very ordinary house.

Of course you had to count the cases that had not got as far as the court, and which probably formed the majority.

Then there was another class of clients, those for whom Jean-Charles Gaillard prepared income tax returns, as he did for Boulay.

Maigret felt sick. He was hot. He was thirsty. It seemed to him that he was getting nowhere and he was tempted to start again from scratch.

"Get me the Tax Inspector for the Ninth Arrondissement . . ."

This was like a shot in the dark, but, at the point where he was, he had no right to neglect anything.

"What's that? . . . Monsieur Jubelin? All right, put me through to Monsieur Jubelin . . . from Chief Superintendent Maigret . . . Yes, of Police Headquarters . . . Hello . . . No, the Chief Superintendent wants to speaks to Monsieur Jubelin in person . . ."

The inspector must have been a busy man, or else very conscious of his own importance, for it took nearly five minutes to get through to him.

"Hello . . . I'm putting you through to the Chief Inspector . . ."

Maigret grabbed the receiver with a sigh.

"I'm terribly sorry to bother you, Monsieur Jubelin. I just want to ask you for a piece of information . . . What's that? . . . Yes, it's indirectly connected with Émile Boulay . . . You've read the papers . . . I see . . . No, it isn't his income tax returns I'm interested in. I might be, later, but in that case I promise you that I shall go through the usual administrative channels . . . Yes, of course, I understand your scruples . . .

"My question is rather different. Did Boulay have any difficulties with you? . . . Yes, that's what I mean . . . Did you ever have occasion, for example, to threaten him with prosecution . . . No? That's what I thought . . . All his accounts perfectly in order . . . I see . . . I see . . ."

He listened, nodding his head and scribbling on his blotting pad. Monsieur Jubelin's voice was so loud that Lucas could hear practically everything he was saying.

"In short, he had a good adviser . . . A lawyer, I know . . . Jean-Charles Gaillard. As it happens, it was about him that I wanted to ask you. I suppose he looked after the affairs of several taxpayers of yours? . . . What's that you say . . . of far too many?"

Maigret winked at Lucas and summoned up his reserves of patience, for the inspector had suddenly become extremely voluble.

"Yes . . . Yes . . . very clever, obviously . . . What? . . . Irreproachable returns . . . You tried to contest them? . . . Without success . . . I see. May I ask you one more question? To what class did most of Gaillard's clients belong? . . . A bit of everything, I see . . . Yes . . . Yes . . . a lot of people from his district . . . proprietors of hotels, restaurants, and night clubs . . . Yes, obviously, it's difficult . . ."

This lasted another ten minutes or so, but soon the Chief Superintendent was listening with only half an ear, for his interlocutor, so reticent to begin with, had begun describing in great detail his fight against tax evaders.

"Whew!" he sighed as he replaced the receiver. "You heard that?"

"Not all of it . . ."

"As I had expected, Émile Boulay's returns were irreproachable. Jubelin repeated that word heaven knows how many times with a sort of nostalgia. For years he had been trying to catch him out. Only last year, he went through all his accounts with a fine-tooth comb without being able to find a single flaw in them."

"And the others?"

"The same is true of all Jean-Charles Gaillard's clients."

Maigret looked thoughtfully at the list drawn up by the inspector. He remembered the clerk's remark:

"He knows how to pick his cases . . ."

Now, in the fiscal domain, too, the lawyer knew how to pick his clients: hotel owners in Montmartre and elsewhere who let their rooms, not only by the night, but by the hour, barkeepers like Jo the Wrestler, night-club proprietors, and race-horse owners . . .

As Jubelin had said a little earlier over the telephone:

"With people like that, it's difficult to furnish proof of receipts and overheads . . ."

Standing at his desk, Maigret looked down the list once again. He had to choose, and possibly the rest of the investigation depended on the choice he made.

"Get me Dupeu . . ."

The inspector came back into the office.

"Do you know what has become of Gaston Mauran, the man you were talking about just now?"

"A month or two ago I caught sight of him at the gas station of a garage on Avenue d'Italie . . . quite by accident. I was driving my wife and kids into the country and I was wondering where I was going to fill up . . ."

"Go and phone the garage proprietor to check whether

Mauran is still working there. But he isn't to say anything to him. I don't want him to take fright and do the disappearance act."

If it did not work with this man, he would pick another, then another, and so on until he had found what he was looking for.

Now, what he was looking for was not very clear. In all the lawyer's cases there was a certain characteristic, a common feature that he would have been hard put to define.

"*A lawyer doesn't kill his clients . . .*"

"Do you need me any longer, Chief?"

"Yes, stay here . . ."

He spoke as if he were talking to himself, not displeased at having an audience.

"When you come to think of it, they all had good reason to be grateful to him. Either they appeared in court and were acquitted, or else the Tax Inspector was obliged to accept their returns. I don't know if you see what I'm getting at . . . A lawyer, in the ordinary run of things, is bound to have a few dissatisfied clients. If he loses a case, if his client is stung by the Tax Inspector . . ."

"I see, Chief . . ."

"Well, it isn't easy to make a choice . . ."

Dupeu came back.

"He's still working at the same garage. He's there now . . ."

"Go and take a car from the yard and bring him here as quickly as you can. Don't scare him. Tell him it's just a question of checking up on a few details. But I don't want him to feel too confident either. . . ."

It was half past four and the heat was not abating. On the contrary, the air was stagnant. Maigret's shirt was beginning to stick to his body.

"How about going for a drink?"

A brief break at the Brasserie Dauphine while they were waiting for Gaston Mauran.

Just as the two men were on the point of leaving the office, the telephone rang. The Chief Superintendent hesitated before turning back, but finally, to satisfy his conscience, he picked up the receiver.

"Is that you, Chief? Torrence speaking . . ."

"I can recognize your voice. Well?"

"I'm speaking to you from the Avenue de la Grande-Armée."

"What are you doing there?"

"About twenty minutes ago, Gaillard came out of his house and got into his car. Luckily a traffic jam at the corner of Rue Blanche gave me time to jump into mine and catch up with him."

"He didn't notice that he was being followed?"

"No, definitely not . . . you'll see in a moment why I'm so sure. He headed immediately for the Étoile, taking the shortest route. The traffic didn't allow him to drive fast, and on the Avenue de la Grande-Armée he slowed down even more. I drove behind him past several garages. He seemed to be hesitating. Finally he drove the car into the Garage Moderne, near Porte Maillot. I waited outside. It was only when I saw him come out on foot and walk in the direction of the Bois that I went in . . ."

This was precisely the tiny unexpected element that was going to rob Maigret of his freedom of action, or, to be more exact, force him to act at a certain moment, in a certain way that he had not foreseen.

His face, while he was listening to Torrence, became increasingly serious, and he seemed to have forgotten the glass of beer he had promised himself.

"It's a big place, with an automatic system for washing cars. I had to show my badge to the foreman. . . . Jean-Charles Gaillard isn't a regular customer . . . they don't remember seeing him before at the garage. He had asked if they could wash his car in an hour at the outside. He said he'd call back about half past five . . ."

"Have they begun the job?"

"They were going to, but I asked them to wait . . ."

He had to make a decision right now.

"What shall I do?"

"Stay there and prevent them from touching the car. I'll send somebody over to bring it here. Don't worry . . . he'll have the necessary papers."

"And when Gaillard comes back?"

"You'll have an inspector with you . . . I don't know yet who it will be. I'd rather there were two of you. You'll be very polite, but you'll make sure all the same that he accompanies you here . . ."

He suddenly remembered the young car thief he was expecting.

"Don't bring him straight into my office . . . Keep him waiting . . . He'll probably get on his high horse . . . don't take any notice. . . . Above all, don't let him get near a telephone."

Torrence sighed unenthusiastically:

"All right, Chief . . . but hurry up. In this heat I would be surprised if he spent a long time walking about the Bois."

Maigret wondered for a moment whether to go straight to the examining magistrate to get sanction for what he was doing. But he was practically certain that the magistrate would prevent him from acting according to his instinct.

In the adjoining office he looked at the inspectors one after the other.

"Vacher . . ."

"Yes, Chief . . ."

"Have you ever driven an American car?"

"Once or twice . . ."

"Go over to the Garage Moderne, on the Avenue de la Grande-Armée. It's right at the bottom, near Porte Maillot. You'll find Torrence there, and he'll show you a blue car. Bring it here and leave it in the yard, touching it as little as possible."

"I get you . . ."

"You, Janin, you'll go with him, but you'll stay at the garage with Torrence. I've given him instructions . . ."

He looked at his watch. It was only a quarter of an hour since Dupeu had left for the Avenue d'Italie. He turned to Lucas.

"Come along . . ."

Provided they did not take long, they were still entitled to their beer.

8

Before having the mechanic brought in, Maigret questioned Dupeu.

"How did it go?"

"At first he seemed surprised and asked me if I worked with you. He struck me as more intrigued than worried. Twice he said:

"'You're sure it's Chief Superintendent Maigret who wants to see me?'

"Then he went to wash his hands with gasoline and took off his overalls. On the way he asked me only one question:

"'Have they any right to reopen a case that has been tried?'"

"What did you reply?"

"That I didn't know, but I supposed not. All the way here, he remained puzzled."

"Bring him in and leave us alone."

Mauran would have been very surprised, as he was being shown into the office, had he known that the famous Chief Superintendent was more nervous than he was. A gawky young man with tousled red hair, china-blue eyes, and freckles around his nose, he looked at Maigret curiously.

"The other times," he began, as if he wanted to get the first blow in, "you left it to your inspectors to question me. . . ."

There was a certain craftiness in him and at the same time a kind of innocence.

"I'd better tell you right off that I've done nothing . . ."

He was not afraid. True, it impressed him to find himself face to face with the big chief, but he was not afraid.

"You're pretty sure of yourself . . ."

"Why shouldn't I be? The court found me not guilty, didn't it? Anyway, practically not guilty. And I played the game . . . you know that more than anybody."

"You mean you gave the names of your accomplices?"

"They had taken advantage of my innocence, the lawyer proved that. . . . He explained that I'd had a difficult childhood, that I had to support my mother, that she was ill . . ."

While he was talking, Maigret had a curious impression. The mechanic was expressing himself with a certain affectation, exaggerating his Parisian accent; at the same time there was an amused sparkle in his eyes, as if he were pleased with the part he was playing.

"I don't suppose you've sent for me about that business? Since then, I've been on my best behavior, and I'd like to see the fellow who could say any different. . . . Well, then?"

He sat down without being invited to do so, which was a rare occurrence, and even took a pack of Gauloises out of his pocket.

"May I smoke?"

And Maigret, watching him all the time, nodded.

"And what if, for some reason or other, we reopened the case?"

Mauran gave a start, uneasy all of a sudden.

"That isn't possible . . ."

"Suppose there are a few points I want to clear up . . ."

The telephone on Maigret's desk suddenly rang and Torrence's voice said:

"He's here . . ."

"Did he protest?"

"Not very much. He says he's in a hurry and wants to see you immediately."

"Tell him I'll see him as soon as I'm free . . ."

Gaston listened, frowning, as if wondering what sort of trick was being played on him.

"It's all an act, isn't it?" he said when the Chief Superintendent had replaced the receiver.

"What's an act?"

"Bringing me here . . . trying to frighten me. . . . You know perfectly well that everything's fixed up."

"What's fixed up?"

"I'm speaking clearly, aren't I? Nobody kicks me around any more."

At that moment, not without a certain awkwardness, he gave a wink, which puzzled Maigret more than all the rest.

"Listen, Mauran. It was Inspector Dupeu who was in charge of your case . . ."

"The fellow who's just brought me in, yes . . . I'd forgotten his name. He was all right."

"What do you mean, all right?"

"He was all right, that's all."

"In what way?"

"Don't you get me?"

"You mean that he didn't set any traps for you and that he questioned you gently?"

"I reckon he questioned me like he was supposed to question me."

Behind the words, in the young man's attitude, there was something ambiguous. The Chief Superintendent tried to pin it down.

"He had to, didn't he?"

"Because you were innocent?"

Mauran, for his part, seemed to be becoming uneasy, as if he were losing track, and as if Maigret's words were

127

baffling him as much as his were baffling the detective.

"Look, . . ." he said hesitantly, after drawing on his cigarette.

"What?"

"Nothing . . ."

"What were you going to say?"

"I've forgotten. . . . Why did you send for me?"

"What were you going to say?"

"It seems to me there's something wrong here . . ."

"I don't understand . . ."

"You're sure? In that case I'd better keep my trap shut . . ."

"It's a bit late to do that. . . . What were you going to say?"

Maigret was not threatening but firm. Standing against the light, he formed a solid mass that Gaston Mauran was beginning to consider with a sort of panic.

"I want to go," he stammered, suddenly standing up.

"Not before you've talked."

"So this is a trap, is it? What's gone wrong? . . . Is there somebody in the racket who hasn't kept the bargain?"

"What bargain?"

"First of all, tell me what you know . . ."

"I ask the questions here . . . What bargain?"

"You'll go on repeating that to me till tomorrow if necessary, won't you? I was told that, but I didn't believe it . . ."

"What else were you told?"

"That they'd let me off lightly . . ."

"Who told you that?"

The young man turned his head away, determined to say nothing, but sensing that he would end up by giving way.

"This isn't fair," he finally muttered between his teeth.

"What isn't?"

Then Mauran suddenly lost his temper, and, getting on

his high horse, looked the Chief Superintendent in the eyes.

"You know very well, don't you . . . And what about the thousand francs?"

He was so taken aback by Maigret's face that his arms fell to his sides. He saw the imposing mass advancing toward him, and two powerful hands, which stretched out and seized him by the shoulders, started shaking him.

Maigret had never been so pale in his life. His face, which was completely expressionless, looked like a block of stone.

His voice, neutral and impressive, issued an order.

"Say that again!"

"The . . . the . . . You're hurting me . . ."

"Say that again!"

"The thousand francs . . ."

"What thousand francs?"

"Let go of me . . . I'll tell you everything . . ."

Maigret released his hold on him, but he remained deathly pale, and at one moment he put his hand on his chest where his heart was pounding wildly.

"I suppose I've been had . . ."

"Gaillard?"

Mauran nodded.

"He promised you that we'd let you off lightly?"

"Yes. He didn't use those words . . . he said you'd be understanding . . ."

"And that you'd be acquitted?"

"That at the worst I'd be put on probation."

"He made you pay him a thousand francs to defend you?"

"Not to defend me . . . It was extra . . ."

"To pass on to somebody else?"

The young mechanic was so overawed that tears came into his eyes.

"To you..."

Maigret stood motionless for two full minutes, his fists clenched; finally a little color gradually returned to his face.

Suddenly he turned his back on his caller, and, although the blind was drawn, he stood a little longer in front of the window.

When he turned around, he had practically regained his usual expression, but Mauran would have sworn that he had aged, that he was suddenly very tired.

He went and sat down at his desk, motioned toward a chair, and mechanically started filling a pipe.

"Smoke..."

He said that as an order, as if to exorcise heaven knows what demons.

Softly, in a quiet, subdued voice, he went on:

"I suppose you're telling the truth..."

"I swear on my mother's head that I am."

"Who sent you to Jean-Charles Gaillard?"

"An old man who lives on Boulevard de la Chapelle."

"Don't be frightened... your case won't be reopened. You're talking about a certain Potier who runs a junk shop..."

"Yes..."

"You did a bit of stealing and passed the stolen goods to him..."

"It didn't happen often..."

"What did he say to you?"

"To go and see that lawyer..."

"Why him rather than another?"

"Because he was in league with the police. I can see now that that isn't true. He swindled me out of a thousand francs."

Maigret reflected.

"Listen. In a moment somebody will be brought into this office. You won't speak to him. You will simply look

130

at him and then accompany the inspector into the next room."

"I'm sorry. You know . . . I'd been told that that's the way things are done. . . ."

Maigret managed to smile at him.

"Hello . . . Torrence? Will you bring him over? I've got somebody in my office I'd like you to keep over there in case I need him again . . . Yes, right now."

He drew on his pipe, outwardly completely calm, but there was a sort of lump in his throat. He fixed his eyes on the door that was going to open, and which did open; he saw the lawyer, a smart figure in a light-gray suit, take two or three quick steps, looking irritable, open his mouth to speak, to protest, and then suddenly catch sight of Gaston Mauran.

Torrence could understand nothing of this silent scene. Jean-Charles Gaillard had stopped short. His face had changed expression. The young man, very ill at ease, rose from his chair and, without looking at the newcomer, walked toward the door.

The two men were left alone, face to face. Maigret, both hands lying flat on the desk, was struggling not to get up, not to walk deliberately toward his vistior, and, although the latter was taller and heavier than himself, not to slap him across both cheeks.

Instead, he said in a curiously weak voice:

"Sit down . . ."

He must have been even more awe-inspiring than when he had pounced on the young mechanic, for the lawyer obeyed automatically, forgetting to protest at the removal of his car and at the fact that two inspectors had brought him without a warrant to the Quai des Orfèvres, where they had kept him waiting like any common suspect.

"I suppose," Maigret began wearily, as if, for him, the

case were closed, "you have understood the situation . . ."

And, as the lawyer tried to reply, he went on:

"Let me do the talking. I shall be as brief as possible, because I find it unpleasant remaining alone with you . . ."

"I don't know what that boy . . ."

"I told you to keep quiet. I didn't have you brought here to question you. I'm not going to ask you for any explanations. If I had obeyed my first impulse, I should have sent you to the Depot without seeing you, and you would have waited there for the results of the investigation."

He pulled toward him List No. 3, that of Gaillard's clients who had appeared in court and had been acquitted or given light sentences.

He read out the names in a monotonous voice, as if he were reciting a litany. Then, raising his head, he added:

"I need hardly say that these people will be questioned. Some of them will keep quiet, or rather, they will begin by keeping quiet. When they learn that the sums they paid over for a definite purpose never reached their destination . . ."

Gaillard's expression had changed, too. All the same, he tried to put up a fight, and started a sentence:

"I don't know what that young scoundrel . . ."

Then Maigret struck the table a blow that made all the objects on it jump into the air.

"Shut up!" he roared. "I forbid you to open your mouth until I ask you to speak . . ."

They had heard the sound of the blow in the inspectors' room, and they all looked at one another.

"I don't need to explain to you how you worked it. And I understand now why you picked your clients carefully. Knowing that they would be acquitted or given a light sentence, you found it easy to make them believe that in return for a fee . . ."

No! He could not talk about that any more.

"I have every reason to believe that my name wasn't the only one you used . . . You looked after people's income tax returns . . . Just now I got in touch with Monsieur Jubelin and I shall be having a long talk with him . . ."

His hand was still trembling slightly when he lighted his pipe.

"It will be a long, tricky investigation. What I can tell you now is that it will be carried out with exemplary care."

Gaillard had stopped glaring at him defiantly and had lowered his head, his hands on his knees, with a gap where the four fingers of the left hand were missing.

The Chief Superintendent's gaze fell on that hand and he hesitated for a moment.

"When the case goes to the Assizes, your counsel will plead your conduct during the war, and probably also your marriage to a woman accustomed to a brilliant life, and the illness that, to all intents and purposes, cut her off from society . . ."

He leaned back in his armchair and closed his eyes.

"Extenuating circumstances will be put forward. Why did you need so much money when your wife no longer went out and you apparently led a lonely life, devoted to work? I don't know and I'm not asking you . . .

"Other people will ask you all these questions, and perhaps you understand why . . . This is the first time, Monsieur Gaillard, that . . ."

His voice failed once more and, without any false shame, he went over to the cupboard and took the bottle of brandy and a glass. This bottle was not there for him but for those who, in the course of a long and tense interrogation, needed it.

He drained the glass at one draft, returned to his seat, and lighted his pipe, which had gone out.

He was a little calmer and spoke now in a casual tone, as if the case no longer concerned him.

"At this very moment, experts are going over your car with a fine-tooth comb. I am not telling you anything new when I say that if it has been used to carry a corpse, there is a good chance that that corpse has left traces behind. You are so well aware of that that after my call this morning you felt the need to have it washed . . .

"Don't say anything! For the last time I order you to keep quiet, otherwise you'll be taken immediately to a cell in the Depot.

"I must also tell you that a team of specialists are on their way to Rue La Bruyère."

Gaillard gave a start and stammered:

"My wife . . ."

"They aren't going there to bother your wife. This morning, looking out of the window, I noticed a sort of shed in the yard. It will be examined inch by inch . . . the cellar, too. And the rest of the house, all the way up to the attic if need be. This evening I shall question your two servants . . . I said don't talk!

"The counsel you choose will have no difficulty in showing that there was no premeditation . . . The fact that your car happened to be out of action, and that you had no other means of transport to get rid of the body, proves that. You had to wait to get the car back and it can't have been very pleasant spending two days and three nights with a corpse in the house."

He ended up by talking to himself, without so much as a glance at the other man. All the little details he had collected during the last few days came back to him and put themselves in their places. All the questions he had asked himself found an answer.

"Mazotti was killed on May 17 and we questioned all the people who had recently been victims of his racket.

At least one of your clients, Émile Boulay, received a pre-liminary summons . . .

"Probably he got in touch with you right away, since you looked after his financial affairs and had intervened in two other, rather unimportant matters . . .

"He accordingly came here on May 18, and he was asked the usual questions.

"After that he was summoned a second time, on the twenty-second or twenty-third. I don't know why . . . probably because Inspector Lucas wanted to ask him for some further details. . . .

"Now it was on the twenty-second, in the afternoon, that Boulay went to the bank to draw five thousand francs. He urgently needed some cash. He couldn't wait until the evening to take it out of the till in one of his night clubs . . .

"And we have found no sign of that sum anywhere . . .

"I'm not asking if it was you who received it . . . I know it was."

He said these last words with a contempt such as he had never shown any human being before.

"On the eighth or ninth of June, Boulay received a third summons for Wednesday the twelfth. He took fright, be-cause he was terrified of scandal. In spite of his profession, or perhaps precisely because of his profession, he clung above all else to his respectability. . . .

"On the evening of June 11, the day before he was due to come here, he was worried, and furious, too, for he had paid five thousand francs as the price of his peace of mind. . . .

"At ten o'clock that night he started calling your house, but without success. He telephoned several times, and, when you finally replied, you agreed to see him a quarter of an hour or half an hour later.

"It is easy to imagine what he said to you in the privacy of your study. He had paid so as not to get mixed up in

135

the Mazotti case, so as to keep his name out of the papers . . .

"Instead of leaving him alone, as he had every right to expect, the police were insisting on questioning him again, and, in the corridors at Police Headquarters, he risked meeting journalists and photographers.

"He felt that he had been deceived. He was as indignant as Gaston Mauran was just now. He told you that he was going to speak his mind and remind the police of the bargain he had made with them.

"That's all . . .

"If he left your house alive, if he came here the next morning and poured out his grievances . . .

"The rest doesn't concern me, Monsieur Gaillard. I have no desire to hear your confession."

He picked up the receiver.

"Torrence? You can let him go . . . Don't forget to get his address, because the examining magistrate will need to see him. Then come and get the individual in my office."

He waited, standing up, impatient to be rid of the lawyer's presence.

Then the latter, his head bowed, murmured in a barely audible voice:

"Have you never had a passion, Monsieur Maigret?"

He pretended not to have heard.

"I have had two . . ."

The Chief Superintendent preferred to turn his back on him, quite determined not to allow himself to be moved.

"First my wife, whom I tried to make happy in every possible way . . ."

His voice was bitter. A silence followed.

"Then, when she was confined to her room and I felt

the need to amuse myself in spite of everything, I found gambling..."

Footsteps sounded in the corridor. There was a gentle knock on the door.

"Come in!"

Torrence stood in the doorway.

"Take him to the back office until I get back from the courthouse."

He did not watch Gaillard leave. When he picked up the receiver, it was to ask the examining magistrate if he could receive him at once.

A short while later, he went through the little glass door that separates the domain of the police from that of the magistrates.

He was away from Police Headquarters for an hour. When he came back, he was holding an official paper in his hand. He opened the door of the inspectors' room and found Lucas impatient for news.

Without any explanation, he handed him the warrant made out in the name of Jean-Charles Gaillard.

"He's in the back office with Torrence. The two of you will take him to the Depot."

"Shall we handcuff him?"

That was the regulation procedure, to which there were a few exceptions. Maigret did not want to appear vindictive. The lawyer's last words were beginning to disturb him.

"No."

"What shall I tell the warder? To take away his tie, his belt, his shoelaces?"

More regulations, and more exceptions!

Maigret hesitated, shook his head, and remained alone in his office.

When he came home to dinner that evening, somewhat

later than usual, Madame Maigret noticed that his eyes were shining and rather fixed, and that his breath smelled of alcohol.

He scarcely opened his mouth during the meal, and he got up to switch off the television. which was annoying him.

"Are you going out?"

"No."

"Is your case over?"

He made no reply.

He had a restless night, got up feeling bad-tempered, and decided to walk to the Quai des Orfèvres, as he sometimes did.

He had scarcely entered his office before the door of the inspectors' room opened. Lucas, with a grave, mysterious expression, closed it behind him.

"I've got some news for you, Chief . . ."

Did he guess what the inspector was going to say? Lucas always asked himself this question and never knew the answer.

"Jean-Charles Gaillard has hanged himself in his cell."

Maigret did not flinch, did not open his mouth, but just stood there looking out the open window at the rustling foliage of the trees, the boats gliding along the Seine, and the passers-by swarming like ants across the Pont Saint-Michel.

"I haven't any details yet . . . Do you think that . . .?"

"Do I think what?" asked Maigret, suddenly aggressive.

And Lucas, beating a retreat, said:

"I was wondering . . ."

He shut the door hard and it was only an hour later that a relaxed Maigret appeared, apparently preoccupied with routine matters.